AF431379

SON OF A WITCH

WICKED WITCHES OF PENDLE ISLAND BOOK 4

MARA WEBB

"*J*uh, have to go," Deacon said at once.

My wand fell from his hand and clattered across the kitchen floor. I stood frozen, unable to process what was happening. Deacon, my lovely human boyfriend and Sheriff of Pendle Island, had just found out I was a witch.

I watched helplessly as he quickly walked out of the kitchen, heading for the front door. It took a second to compose myself. I had to stop him, I had to explain myself. Who knew what he was going through right now?

"Deacon, wait!" I said, hurrying out of the kitchen and into the hallway. He quickly opened the front door and skipped down the porch stairs. "Please, I can explain!"

"I have to go!" he said. "Bye! Don't follow me!"

I wasn't sure what mood Deacon was in. He didn't seem angry or mad, just... shocked.

"Please!" I said, stopping at the edge of the porch. Not only had Deacon just discovered that I'd been hiding a huge secret in our relationship, but he'd also just learned that magic was real. "You can't tell anyone!" I blurted out. As if that mattered.

Deacon climbed into his cruiser and quickly reversed away from the house and sped down the driveway back down to the main road. I let out a long frustrated sigh and ran my fingers through my hair. Turning back, I saw Old Mad John, the pirate ghost who haunted my house. He was lingering in the front door, his ghostly fingers curled around the frame.

"Get out?" he asked, offering the words in a sympathetic way that suggested *is everything okay?* The poor pirate ghost could only say two words for some reason, but he adjusted his tone when he was trying to say something else.

"No, everything is *not* okay," I said, my voice clipped with frustration. It seemed that living on this island was like fighting a hydra. Every time I solved one problem another two cropped up in its place.

"Not to be a drag," Selena said as she also came into the doorway to see what was happening, "but Adam really does need your help."

I had known Selena for about three minutes. She was a witch, like me, but her magic was a little different to mine. She was a Therian, which basically meant she had the ability to shift into the form of animals. For a long time, a legendary puma had stalked the island. Since moving here, I figured it was a yarn to get tourists in, which it did, but I came home tonight to find a puma lying on my table.

That same puma had shifted into the form of Selena, who informed me that my gardener, Adam, was in mortal danger.

"Look I've had a very crazy week," I said looking up at the sky. "Can't I just, I don't know, have a nice quiet week before things get all mental again?"

Out of the corner of my eye I saw Selena and Old Mad John looking at one another, the expression on their faces suggesting I was crazy. Yes, standing in the presence of a pirate ghost and a puma shifter. *I* was the crazy one.

"Who's she talking to?" Selena whispered to Old Mad John. The pirate ghost just shrugged and whispered back his trademark two words, which I took to mean, *beats me.*

"Oh, I'm just praying to the witchy gods," I said as I looked back at the pair standing in my doorway. "If such a thing exists."

"They exist all right!" Selena said. "They're goddesses by the way.

All of them. There's like a hundred. Kind of like the Greek gods? The main one is called Avalon, she's the goddess of Contempt and Plaited Breads, then there's her first sister, Fayka, she's the god—"

"Wow, I really don't have time for this right now," I said. "Didn't you say something about Adam's life being in danger?"

"Right." Selena nodded. "Sorry, I get carried away with my witchy mythology. The thing with Adam, how much do you know about him? I know he's a mysterious character, but I mean, how well do you actually—"

"I know he's a werewolf, if that's what we're getting at," I said.

"Ah, good, well that saves some time. Adam has got himself into trouble with a werewolf coven that lives out on the west side of the island. They seem to think he has taken something from them, and they are currently holding him prisoner until he confesses."

"What?!"

"Yes, as you can see the situation is not ideal, but if it's any consolation I think he is guilty."

I shook my head as I tried to decipher the non-stop stream of crazy that was my life. "What do they think he stole?"

"An ancient artifact, some sort of cup or something. I'm a little hazy on the details, I was in my puma form for an awful long time."

Selena actually didn't seem overly concerned about the whole taken-prisoner-by-werewolves thing. "I'm just having a hard time processing this. It sounds pretty urgent, but you're pretty laid back about it all. Is he in danger or not?"

"Um… not immediate. But if he doesn't return this cup soon, they will probably, you know," Selena mimed slicing a finger across her neck and stuck her tongue out, as if this was all some lovely game of charades. "I shifted out of my puma form and came to find you for help, so that's something. I don't go back to my human form for any old reason."

So, this was serious. I mean, it didn't sound like a stroll in the park on a Sunday. He was being held prisoner; I couldn't imagine that was anything other than bad.

"How do we find them?" I asked.

"They have this little hidey hole, this magical clearing. Only were-wolves can get in and out, but there's a gate that opens every night for five minutes at midnight. You can go there and plead your case to get in."

"Can't you shift into a wolf or something and sneak us in?"

"First of all," Selena said, "I'm not doing any sort of sneaking around werewolves. Those guys can get awfully territorial. Second of all, I've been doing the puma thing for so long that I'm not sure I can do anything else. Go pumas!" she said, hoisting a celebratory fist into the air.

I was still trying to get a pulse on Selena. When she first appeared on my kitchen table, she seemed like some sort of mysterious seductress. But the more she talked I got the impression she was some sort of goofball joker type, always cracking jokes to cover up her own nervousness. A quick glance at my watch revealed it was only thirty minutes to midnight.

"Is half an hour enough time to get there from here?"

"Probably not," she said. "But we can go and visit tomorrow. Like I said, they're probably not going to kill him anytime soon. He did take that cup, and they *really* want it back."

"None of this makes any sense," I said. "Adam is a good guy. He's not a thief."

"I'm not disputing he's a good guy, but I'm almost certain I saw him running through the woods with that cup in his little wolfy mouth. What's your shower like by the way?"

"My what?"

"Your shower. You know. Good water pressure?"

"It used to be bad, but it's better now. Why?"

"Well I figured I'd stay for a few days. I feel like I'm not going back into puma form anytime soon, and I don't have a house on the island anymore. Looks like you've got plenty of room up here. What do you say? Quid pro quo. Room for board?"

A lodger was really the last thing I needed at the moment, but I didn't exactly want to cart Selena out on the street, especially as she had only just transformed back into her human form. "Uh, look, you can stay for a bit if you need to. You don't have to work or anything, just make sure you clean up after yourself."

Selena batted a hand dismissively. "Forget that, I've spent long enough lazing around in puma form. I'm looking forward to getting to work and earning my way! You're missing a groundskeeper, right? I can help mow the lawn and look after the gardens until we get Adam back!"

"Get out," Old Mad John added calmly. I wasn't exactly sure what he meant this time, but he had a big smile on his face, and the words were calm and welcoming. I think maybe it was *let's go inside for a cup of tea.*

We all made our way inside and I tried to figure out how this pretty good day had already ended in a spectacularly terrible fashion. I gave Selena a quick tour of the house and told her to help herself to food and whatever else she needed. Her eyes lit up when she discovered there was a bath in the en-suite of the guest room.

"Oh, I haven't bathed properly in so long! I'm going to have a nice soak and I'll see you in the morning!"

It was late, and I usually would have gone to bed by now myself, but for some reason I found myself restless. I went back downstairs and found my familiar, Artemis, on the kitchen table with his head in an open container of ice cream. The little black cat either didn't hear me enter or didn't care.

"So that's where all the ice cream is going," I said.

Artemis snapped his head up, seemingly startled by my presence. "Alofax! Oh, god, it's just you, Chelsea. I thought you went to bed."

"No, I was giving Selena a tour of the house. That's the puma woman. She's going to be staying with us for a few days. She's in the guest room, so stay out of there and give her some privacy."

"The guest room? But that's where I do some of my best singing! Ugh. Fine. I'll respect her boundaries, or whatever. What are you still doing up this late?"

"I guess I'm worrying about this Deacon thing. He knows I'm a witch, and he knows about magic too. What happens now? You're my familiar right, you should advise me on this sort of thing."

"Well first of all I finish eating this ice cream, then I wash myself for fifteen minutes and then I fall asleep for ten to fifteen hours."

"Come on man," I said, desperation evident in my voice. "I actually really need help for once. What do I do?"

Artemis regretfully pushed the ice cream to one side and licked away the creamy little beard dripping around his mouth. "I'll help you on one condition. Get chocolate fudge flavor next time. Who even buys birthday cake flavor ice cream?"

"I do," I said. "I like it."

"Chocolate fudge or I leave you to wallow in your misery."

"You're the worst familiar ever, but okay, we have a deal. What do I do? How badly have I messed up?"

Artemis took a huge breath of air as though he was about to deliver some terrible news. I braced myself. The little cat did have a penchant for drama, but he was overly dramatic most of the time.

"Look, things are probably going to be okay. I mean, humans aren't really meant to know about our magical kind. But it's not like we round them up and execute them when they find out the secret. Not anymore at least."

"What?!"

"Relax. I'm kidding." He glanced to the side for a second. "Mostly. Anyway. It all depends on how Deacon's going to react. If he starts blabbing about it the MCI will pick it up and send someone in to deal with the leak."

"The MCI?" I let out a long and hearty groan. The MCI or 'Magical Crimes Investigation' was a helplessly disorganized bureaucratic nightmare responsible for solving suspected magical crimes. I'd had a few run ins with them now and they were a headache to say the least. "What do they do?"

"They have a Blanking division. They do small memory wipes on mortals that see magical things, things they aren't meant to see. Their magical systems have probably already detected this slipup, I wouldn't be surprised if someone—"

As if on cue the kitchen filled with bright plumes of pink and green smoke. After Artemis and I finished coughing the smoke cleared to reveal Chad Chaplin. Chad was a lanky young man with big ears and a boyish face. So far he had been my only contact of the MCI. He was clumsy, chaotic and his entrances were quite often disastrous. He also happened to be my magical mentor, though he hadn't been much help there either.

Chad took one look at me and frowned.

"Chelsea Sponks? Good gravy. Please don't tell me there's been another murder."

"No."

"Ah, good! You need help with your studies then?"

As Chad figured his bearings, he pulled out reams and reams of note paper from his coat pockets, much like the endless reams of receipts you get at some drugstores.

"I didn't summon you," I said. "And stop appearing in my house!"

"You know for a junior detective you're pretty dumb," Artemis said dryly to Chad.

"I'm actually a Warlock in Principis now, you talking feather duster. I'm the overseer of all magical enquiry from the west coast of America to the east coast of Russia!"

"Avalon help us all," Artemis muttered under his breath.

"That sounds like quite a significant promotion," I said to Chad.

"Yeah it's a bit of a big leap," he said, his face grey and sweating. Something told me Chad was a little over his head, but I also felt that way when he was just a junior detective. "My uncle is kind of high up in the MCI and he's keen for me to climb the ranks. There's also a shortage of witches and wizards willing to work for the MCI, so if you stick around long enough you just end up getting promoted."

"Wonder why," Artemis said sarcastically.

"Because this organization is like a live grenade!" Chad said, still rummaging through his pockets to try and figure out why he was summoned here. He could have just, I don't know, asked me, or given me a chance to tell him, but that wasn't really Chad's style.

A glass bottle of red liquid tumbled out of his duster pocket and smashed on the floor. The liquid immediately became a dozen tiny red lizards that scattered in every direction.

"What were they?!" I remarked.

"Jazz lizards," Chad said. "Don't worry about it, they're great. They'll evaporate in about two weeks. Do you like jazz?"

"Hate it."

"Uh well… maybe get some earplugs. Ah! Here we are! It looks like I was summoned here for a…" His face dropped. "A blanking? Are you kidding me? You told someone you were a witch?"

"I didn't tell anyone anything. My boyfriend accidentally found out."

"And where is he now?"

"He left. He was a little freaked out."

"Yeah, I wonder why. Well we'll have to keep a close eye on him and see how he reacts. What's his name?"

"Deacon Long. He's the island sheriff."

"Long," Chad said, as though repeating the words to someone else. "Did you get that? Go keep a close eye on him and report back to me."

Both Artemis and I looked at one another. "Are you talking to someone?" I asked.

Chad looked up at me. "Huh? Oh. Yes. Sorry. I forget you can't see them. Weevil, can you show yourself for a second?"

Suddenly a small green sprite appeared. The thing was completely naked, no taller than my knee and had long ears, a pointed nose and its fingers and toes were like twigs.

"Ja?" it said, in a high-pitched voice that had a slight Scandinavian accent.

"This is Weevil," Chad said to me. "He's a Detector. These little guys are the backbone of the MCI. They're all around us, watching and recording us witches and wizards. Weevil and his team will keep an eye on Deacon and evaluate his response. If he's too risky we'll blank him and everyone he talked to since he found out your secret, resetting their memory to an hour before he learned about magic. If he's safe… well. He can keep his memories. I guess we'll have to wait and see what Weevil and his boys find out."

"Watch em!" Weevil said. "Judge em, blank em!"

The little sprite disappeared, leaving me more confused than anything. I had little faith that someone like Chad could fairly judge something as complex as this, now that I knew the entire organization was built off the work of strange little green sprites with broken English, I felt even less secure in my trust.

"He's not in trouble, is he?"

"Your boyfriend? Probably not. You might get some points on your witching license though."

"I don't have a witching license yet!"

"Yeah I know. Doesn't look good does it?" He said with a disinterested smile, leafing through endless notepads from within his jacket. "Anyway, this is a pretty simple one. Weevil and the boys will take care of this. We'll give it a few days and review accordingly. Until then, is there anything else I can help you with?"

"Yeah, can you move me far away from this island? Teleport me somewhere nice and quiet?"

"I'm temporarily banned from teleporting other people around. Poor Esmerelda Firo still wakes up screaming about those badgers."

"…What?"

"Never mind. I just remembered I'm legally not allowed to talk about that. I uh… ah! I have some Morpheus berries if you want a goodnight sleep?" he suggested, pulling a handful of squished berries out of one of his many duster pockets.

"I'll uh… pass, thanks," I said. I had seen firsthand the way those little berries could make a person lose their mind. "I don't want to risk taking too many and go loopy."

"Loopy, that reminds me, can you give this to your cousin Lizzy?" Chad fished around in his jacket and pulled out a small ruby-sequined purse. "She left it at—" He stopped himself. "She left it. Anyway. I have to go," he said, slapping the purse into my hand. "See you in a few days!"

"Wait!" I said, "I—"

I wanted to know if there was anything I could do to help minimize Deacon's chances of getting blanked, but the kitchen was already full of pink and green smoke. Chad was gone.

"He *has* to stop doing that," Artemis said when the smoke was finally clear. "I should put a charm on the house preventing access to anyone that isn't a normal height."

"You're a person in a cat's body," I pointed out. "Wouldn't that rule you out?"

Artemis squinted at me. "Let's just go to bed. And don't forget about that ice cream." He jumped into my arms and I caught him, giving him a little nuzzle on the ear as I headed back upstairs. I wanted to point out that Artemis hadn't actually helped at all, but it would just be easier to get him the ice cream he wanted.

When I finally made it into bed, I was so tired that the stressors of the last hour weren't enough to keep me awake. Artemis curled up around my feet at the bottom of the bed and I found myself drifting off. One final glance at the clock on my bedside table revealed it was nearly one in the morning.

I was going to be tired tomorrow.

Just as my eyes drifted for the final time my cell lit up on the nightstand. I quickly grabbed the buzzing phone and answered.

"Hello?!" I said, partly panicked and confused from being half asleep.

"Chelsea? It's momma! Good news! I'm coming to visit! Got to go, Marco's calling!"

The line went dead and I lay there staring at the bright phone screen. Suddenly a strong nauseous feeling filled my stomach and I felt fraught with nerves.

Mom was coming. To the island?!

I had no chance of falling asleep now.

"Zaza La Who?" I said to Lizzy over our stacks of square-shaped pancakes.

"Zaza LaFoo," she repeated, shoveling a forkful of pancake into her mouth. "He's this artsy type that lives on the island sometimes. Very famous. International profile. He was on the cover of Vogue, and I think he's dating Taylor Swift."

"Who isn't?" I asked.

Lizzy snorted. "Anyway, Zaza is back on the island again. He has a new art exhibit, and he's chosen Pendle Museum as the first stop on his international world tour. Bash's studio is handling the music for the opening night tonight, and I have to go. It's a work thing."

"And that means I have to come why?"

"Because it's a party, it's fun, and I think you need to loosen up a little. Plus, you look like the waking dead. Sleep poorly?"

I swigged down the rest of my coffee and a long yawn escaped me. I was more than a little tired. After my mom called it took me several hours to get back to sleep, and even then, I was tossing and turning. I kept having nightmares about Deacon.

Once I finally did get to sleep, I woke up not long after that to my cell phone ringing once again. It was Lizzy, and she wanted to get a fresh stack of pancakes at one of our favorite breakfast places in town: Aztec Pancake.

Aztec Pancake was this fun little themed-diner, designed to look like a crumbling Aztec ruin. The outside of the diner looked like a miniature Aztec temple, and the theme continued inside too. Fake vines swooped down from the ceiling and the sound of jungle ambiance played over the background of the restaurant.

Even the food was designed on theme. The stacks of pancakes were square and decreased in size with each ascending layer. I was currently cutting apart a pancake Aztec temple, complete with a miniature sacrificial slab on top made from coffee wafer. A solitary raspberry was placed on top of the wafer, the unlucky sacrifice for this sugar-laden meal.

"Top up?" Carmen said as soon as I placed my cup down. I didn't even have to answer. The cup was fill and she was over on the other side of the diner before I could finish yawning. I gratefully took the cup and muttered a sleepy, 'Thanks Carmen,' even though she was already gone. I looked up and saw Lizzy staring at me, one brow raised.

"Huh? What?" I asked. Had she asked me something?

"I asked you if you slept poorly, but I guess I already know the answer. Been having fun with Deacon?"

"Deacon? What? Oh." I put my cup down, picked up my fork and cut off a big old chunk of pancake. "Yeah, not that. I had a pretty bad night last night. It did involve Deacon though."

Lizzy raised both her eyebrows. "Oh no, not drama." She leaned back in her chair and then a giant smile spread across her face. "I love drama! What happened?"

"Gee, where do I begin?" I said. I felt my amethyst locket vibrate around my neck, a sign that Artemis wanted out. I clicked the stone and an astral form of my familiar zapped onto the windowsill next to our booth. It had been raining quite heavily all morning and raindrops streaked the large glass windows at the front of the diner.

"Rain again?" Artemis muttered to himself. "That liar of a weatherman said it was sunny today!" He immediately curled up, looking as though he was promptly about to fall asleep.

I looked away from the astral cat, deciding it was best to ignore him. He was translucent and blue in his astral form, and I was the only one that could see him like this fortunately.

"Skip to the good stuff, ignore the boring parts," Lizzy directed.

"The Pendle puma is not only real, it was in my kitchen last night. On the table of all places."

"The Pendle puma was in your kitchen?"

"It's not really a puma," I said. "It's Selena Merryweather, Astrid's sister. She's a Therian, a shape shifter."

"Why was she in your kitchen?"

"Adam has got himself into trouble with a werewolf pack or something. I don't know. I have to sort that out tonight. Anyway, I turned around and saw Deacon standing behind me. He let himself in with the spare key I gave him. I'd left my wand in the car, of all things."

"Oh, cripes."

"Yeah, *and* he saw Selena transform from a puma into her human form. He knows I'm a witch, and he knows about magic."

Lizzy, a punk-rocker to the core, actually looked stressed out for once. "Chelsea! This is serious! Humans aren't supposed to know about us! Did you use *fuhgeddaboudit* on him?"

'Fuhgeddabouit!' was a spell shouted in your worst Italian accent. I'd seen Lizzy use it once before in this very booth when Carmen noticed another one of Lizzy's magical spells. It zapped the last few seconds of the subject's memory, and if I'd been using my brain it would have actually been super useful last night.

"No, I guess you could say I *forgot about it*." Heh. "Deacon freaked out and left before I could talk to him. I tried calling him a few times this morning, but he's not answering."

"Sounds like he's freaking all right. What happens now? I've never had this problem before."

"It's the MCI's business now apparently. Chad showed up in my kitchen and said Deacon was under investigation. He has this whole team of little invisible pixie men following him around."

"Detectors? Yeah, they're everywhere. There's literally almost an infinite amount of them. The MCI is largely useless, but they somehow landed an agreement with the Detectors. They report stuff to the MCI and then the MCI send witches and wizards in to solve the crimes. That's how the whole system works."

"Well it makes me uncomfortable," I said. "I wish I could get hold of Deacon and try to calm him down. I don't want Chad or those things messing with his memory. If they decide Deacon is a risk, they'll wipe his memory and the memory of everyone he talks to after he found out the secret."

"Chad is such an idiot," Lizzy said and rolled his eyes. "I wish that telephone pole would stop popping up so much."

Lizzy and Chad had met a few times and always had some choice insults to throw at one another. I didn't think any of it was really mean spirited, it was good-natured ribbing with a side of brutal honesty. It did remind me of something though.

"By the way, breakfast is on me. It's my treat."

Lizzy's face lit up. "Really? Why?"

"For being such a good cousin. You deserve it. You're always honest and never keep any secrets from me."

"Aw, shucks cuz, thanks! You're a babe too."

Her smile dropped as soon as I pulled her ruby-sequined purse from my bag. "Uh… where did you get that?"

"Oh, Chad just happened to hand it to me last night when he *poofed* his way into my kitchen." I handed the purse to Lizzy, who quickly took it and shoved it into her black denim jacket. "Why would he have it?"

"Well, that's a funny story actually," Lizzy said, her eyes darting quickly about. "I was uh… setting off some magical fireworks on the hilltop the other night, they might have been slightly illegal. Anyway, I was minding my own business, not hurting anyone, and would you believe it, that haunted beanpole Chad appeared out of nowhere and issued me a fine for magical mischief!"

"Magical fireworks?" I said.

"Yes."

"What hill?"

"The hill. *The* hill."

"What was so illegal about these fireworks?"

"They were—listen, what's with the third degree here?!"

I sat back in my chair and smiled at my cousin, who was very obviously sweating under my interrogation. It wasn't often I got to turn the screws on Lizzy, normally it was the other way around.

"Just admit you went on a date with him. Why else would he have your purse? You left it behind. Did you stay at his place? Does he have a place? Does he live with his mom?"

"He doesn't live with his mom—" Lizzy started before stopping herself. She realized she had given the game away. She pounded her fist on the table and let out a reproachful moan. "Argh! I hate having a detective for a cousin! I can't keep anything from you!"

"Come on," I said. "Spill the delicious gossip beans. You're dating Chad?!"

"I am *not* dating him," she insisted. "It was one drink, and my story about fireworks was true. I was setting off some fireworks the other night when that malnourished coatrack appeared out of nowhere and scared the bejeezus out of me. He said I could pay the fine for the illegal fireworks or go for a drink with him instead. I must have left my purse in the bar."

"You like him," I said after studying her for a moment.

"That incompetent oaf? Are you kidding? He looks like he's the wrong aspect ratio, and he's terrible at his job!"

"He caught you with those illegal fireworks," I said. "He's not all terrible. Just a little disorganized. He usually helps once he figures out why he's been summoned. Come on, admit it, you like him."

"Is that what he said to you? I was laughing at his jokes because I wanted to get out of there faster. He's not that funny. Not as funny as he thinks."

Lizzy's face was bright red now. I was quickly learning that my cousin was not only terrible under pressure, but also terrible at admitting there might be some sentiment under her hardcore punk rock exterior. I was tempted to sit there and poke fun at her all morning, but my focus quickly broke as my phone buzzed on the table with a new message.

It was a picture message from an unknown number. The picture showed a young and uncomfortable looking Hispanic man holding two thumbs up from a poolside lounger. A caption underneath the picture read, 'Marco said he'd drop me off for my flight!'

"Oh no," I said. Lizzy, eager to shift the conversation rapidly to anything else jumped right in.

"Oh no? What now? Another dead body?"

"Worse," I said. "I got a call from my mother last night. She said she's planning to visit the island."

"Ooh, I love your mom! She's so much fun! When does she get here?!"

"She didn't say. If we're lucky the winds will blow the hounds of hell off course and she'll breeze right past the island."

Lizzy laughed and rolled her eyes. "Come on, she's not that bad. This rock could do with a visit from fun Auntie Lorelai."

"Uh, yeah, have you met my mom since you became an adult? The 'fun' thing gets old fast. If you've really got any feelings for Chad or any other man on this rock then you better lock the men up, because she will devour them."

My mother had a long and sordid history of being a bit of a man eater. Growing up I never knew who my real father was, but I stood on the sidelines as my mother collected marriages and divorces like they were going out of fashion.

At the last official count, I think she had been divorced fifteen times. I was pretty sure I was in the running for 'person with most step-fathers.'

Growing up I just thought she was some kooky old love hound, but I recently found out her relationship habits were directly related to her magic. Falling in love powered my mother's magic, something she had done to keep food on the table for me. She'd been doing it for so long now that if she stopped her magic would eat her alive, so she had to keep collecting those wedding rings.

"Between your Deacon problem and the call from your mom I'm surprised you got any sleep at all."

"Now you know why I'm so tired," I said.

"You still have to come to this thing tonight," Lizzy said as she wolfed down the last of her pancake. "I only have to do a bit of actual work, and the rest of the night we can have some fun and look at weird art. Apparently this exhibit is key themed. Zaza always takes his themes very seriously. He's a bit pretentious, but he is actually a half-decent artist. Look, here he is now!"

I looked through the diner's front window and saw a small entourage making its way across the front lot of Aztec Pancake. At the center of the group there was a small skinny man with a platinum white bob and large black shades, the type of frames you would see on an old blind woman. He was wearing a turtleneck sweater and a long brown jacket was draped over his shoulders.

A small Asian girl ran behind him carrying a large black umbrella, so he was completely shielded from the rain. At the front there was a large gorilla looking type security man in a tight black t-shirt. At the very rear there was a real housewife type, shielded by another umbrella, also held by the small Asian girl. The statuesque blonde looked far too made-up to be going into a place like Aztec Pancake.

But sure enough they came in. As they did every conversation came to a temporary pause as everyone turned to regard Zaza and his crew. The attention didn't seem to go unnoticed.

"Back to your meals," the gruff security type at the front barked. "No staring."

Aztec Pancake was a small family operation owned by husband and wife, Bo Bennett and Neville Bennet. Bo was rarely seen, she was the one handling all the business behind the curtain. Neville was her husband, a large Jamaican fry cook with a personality to match his jolly demeanor.

"Well it is an honor!" Neville announced proudly from behind the counter. He wiped his pancake batter hands across his apron and came around the front to greet Zaza and his crew. Neville had two volumes. Loud and louder. "Mr. LaFoo! I didn't expect to see you here."

Zaza turned his head slowly, surveying the far corners of the diner like a predatory sloth searching for the perfect leaf. He finally looked back at Neville and nodded gently. "It's tacky, full of poor people and completely and utterly tasteless. I love it." Zaza had a very strong accent, one that I couldn't place at all. Maybe German? I found his opening review a little offensive, but Neville didn't seem bothered.

"Just wait until you try the pancakes," he said. "We have a table over in the far corner if you'd like a little privacy. This way."

"Certainly. Poppy!"

The little Asian woman took Zaza's jacket from off his shoulders and hurried across the diner to follow Neville, rushing right past the booth that Lizzy and I were sitting in. She immediately started wiping down the booth with baby wipes, while a perplexed looking Neville stood to one side waiting for the others to walk over so he could hand out menus.

Zaza slowly walked past, with the statuesque blonde in tow and his huge security guard at the rear.

"This is exactly what I wanted, Verity," Zaza said in his strong german accent as he swanned past us. "To be among the rabble, to live amongst the knuckle dragging dwellers that reside upon this fine rock, you know, the island is breathtakingly beautiful, but some of the local inhabitants…"

Zaza's drivel faded out of earshot as he walked to their table in the far corner. Lizzy and I stared at one another. I glanced across the restaurant and saw equal expressions of bafflement on the other diner's faces.

"Quite an entrance," I said to Lizzy as everyone started to talk amongst themselves again.

"Yeah, he really comes across as likeable," Lizzy said sarcastically.

"Someone needs to take the broom out of that guys butt and clean up his mouth!" Artemis remarked. It was probably a good thing I was the only one that could hear and see him.

"He seems delightful," I said to Lizzy, reaching for another much-needed swig of coffee. "Not exactly inspiring me to come to this show tonight. What a snob!"

"He's a rich snob, and he brings a lot of money to the island. Come on. It'll be fun. He is a complete jerk, but his art is actually pretty good. Besides, what else do you have going on?"

"Apart from springing Adam from a pack of hostile werewolves? Not much."

"Ah he'll be fine! Do you really need him anyway?"

"Do you know how big the lawn is at the back of my house? I'm not mowing that myself."

"Get a new gardener," Artemis piped in from the windowsill. "It can't be that hard to mow grass. If that idiot can do it, anyone can."

"Pipe down, Artemis," I whispered to him.

"Look you said you can only go and see these wolves at midnight or something, right? If you come to this show, I'll come and help you out with that after. I've been on this island forever, I've bumped into a few of these shifters, I probably know them!"

"Are they dangerous?"

"Nah. Stupid? Yeah. I'm sure it's all just a big misunderstanding. But I can help."

"Sigh," I said. A sigh on its own didn't seem to cut the mustard. "Just as long as you agree not to abandon me on my own at this art thing."

Lizzy beamed. "Chelsea, you have yourself a deal."

3

"*L*izzy! You promised!"

"It's just for ten minutes, I need to look after the decks while Bash goes to the bathroom! Just enjoy the aperitifs and soak up the art!"

I glared at my cousin as she disappeared into the well-dressed crowd, leaving me alone, three minutes after we arrived at the art show. Pendle museum was a lovely building really, tall palatial ceilings and marble columns. Zaza's art pieces decorated the huge rooms finely. The man was a donkey's ass, of that I had no doubt, but I had to admit his work did have an impressive aesthetic. The theme of this particular exhibit was supposed to be 'keys' and Zaza had made one hundred individual sculptures and pictures from old keys that he had welded together.

The event was black-tie, so the men were all dressed in tuxedos and the women all looked like extras from a bond film. I had on a fancy red cocktail dress, one that I had bought from a thrift shop in Pendle mall only hours earlier. Lizzy left me standing in front of a huge canvas covered in swirling rows of rusted metal keys. It looked like Van Gogh's starry night. The scene depicted a stormy sea.

I sipped at my tall flute of bubbly orange juice and tried my best to fit in, shifting my weight onto one hip as I pretended to contemplate the piece and its inner workings. I heard a minor commotion behind me, which promptly distracted my budding career as an art critic.

"Excuse me, there's a line here!" a well-dressed older man said as a younger man in scruffy-biker gear cut the line at the bar and grabbed two drinks for himself. He didn't seem to notice he had cut in line at all, and if he had noticed, he clearly didn't care.

He was wearing tattered black jeans, an old leather jacket, a stained t-shirt and dog-eared boots. He had unkempt black hair and a few days of stubble. The line-cutter walked away from the bar and downed both the drinks before handing them off to a passing waitress. He took another glass from her tray, along with a handful of aperitifs.

It was pretty obvious from the muddy boot prints and his scruffy attire that this person wasn't meant to be in here, but he didn't seem to care at all. Judging by the way everyone else was looking at him they thought he stood out too. He wolfed down his finger food, walked over to a coatrack by the door and pulled a wallet out of a jacket that almost certainly didn't belong to him.

For some reason I found myself watching his every move now, but the rest of the crowd had seemingly forgot about him. I watched for several minutes as he meandered about the room, scowling at the pieces and displaying as many bad habits as one possibly could.

I walked around myself and came back to the large sea picture, which was titled *Port in a Storm*, when the line-cutter wandered over in my direction and looked up at the huge key-covered canvas. "Avalon be," he said. "This might be the worst one of the lot." I watched in fascination as he started biting his fingernails and spitting them out onto the floor. Avalon? Was this degenerate a wizard?

"I quite like it actually," I said. I was telling the truth. I wasn't sure about the piece at first, but it really was quite impressive the longer you stared at it. I'd done a few laps of the room now and this particular piece was a cut above the rest.

The man scoffed. "I know you. Chelsea Sponks. Seen you in that paper enough times. Solving murders and all that."

"And to who do I owe the pleasure?" I said sarcastically.

"Rudy," he said, snapping his fingers and conjuring up a cigarette. "Rudy Malkin."

My eyes were already wide at Rudy so brazenly performing magic in a public space. He just didn't seem to care at all. His surname was the thing that really caught my attention though. "Malkin? Like Mary Malkin?"

"Third Aunt once removed," Rudy said, taking a long drag of his cigarette. He looked at me and smirked. "Sponks girl, aye? I know all about your family. Troublemakers the lot of you."

"Troublemakers?!" I scoffed. "Have you witnessed any of your behavior in the last five minutes?"

"Don't know what you mean," he said.

"Cutting in line, stealing wallets, using magic in front of humans. Being very… rude!"

He smirked again, taking another long drag of his cigarette. He blew smoke up towards the high ceilings and with another snap of his fingers his cigarette was gone. "What? You think any of these bozos notice stuff like that? Anyone can hide magic, you just have to learn how." He stared at me for a moment. "You're proper green, aren't you?"

"Green?"

"New. I can feel it. Your magic is practically raw. You didn't grow up magical."

"Oh, no. My mom kept it a secret."

"Did she now? I wonder why she did that."

"She had her reasons. Look, I don't mean to be rude or anything, but aren't you a little off the dress code?"

Rudy looked down at his tattered biker clothes. "Scott didn't seem to mind."

"Scott being?"

He nodded over to the door and I turned to see Zaza's head of security, the tank of a man in a black t-shirt that was several sizes too small. "Scott. He runs 'Zaza's' security detail."

"And your good friends with him, are you? Or did you use magic to get past him too?"

"I'm just checking in on the opening night," Rudy said innocuously. "I'm one man appreciating art. I have to see Zaza about something and then I'm gone. I'm washing my hands of all this."

I had no idea what he was talking about, I was just trying to think up an excuse to leave. I was about to head off to find Lizzy when Rudy opened his mouth again. "What do you think this means then?" he said, referring to the stormy key picture in front of us.

"Huh? What? Oh," I looked up at the huge canvas. I had no idea how many keys were used to make this picture, but it had to be thousands easily. The bottom half of the scene showed iron-black waves churning in tall peaks. A rolling grey sky loomed over that, with a tiny circle of sunlight in the top left corner.

"I think to me it means that there's a glimmer of hope, even when things appear to be helplessly dark." Rudy laughed, almost spitting up his drink. "What's funny?" I asked. "That's my opinion."

"It's a stupid opinion," he said. "And obviously wrong."

"How can it be wrong? Art is subjective."

"Nah, you're dead wrong."

"You tell me what it means then."

Rudy adopted a dramatic judgmental pose and then nodded to himself. "Oh yes. It's very obvious," he muttered.

"What?"

"The world is dark, and everything sucks."

"Right."

"And the sea is awesome."

Maybe he thought he was funny, but I just found him very annoying. "I guess we'll check in with Zaza on that one and see what he thinks."

"Oh, I can't imagine he'll know either, much as he might like to waffle on."

I couldn't get over the gall on this guy. "And you know his art better than he does?"

"I never said that," Rudy said. "But I think I know the meaning of this piece better than anyone else."

"And why's that?"

"Because I made it." Rudy handed me his two empty glasses and looked past me. "Hopefully we don't run into each other again Chelsea Sponks, you're dreadfully boring. If you'll excuse me, I have a paycheck to collect."

I watched in shock as Rudy pushed his way through the crowd to corner Zaza's small Asian assistant, Poppy. The pair appeared to share some heated words and then Poppy led Rudy off somewhere out of sight. I was confused as I was insulted, I don't think I'd ever met anyone quite as unlikeable.

"Wow," Lizzy said as she made her way back over to me. "Two empty drinks in ten minutes. Is being away from me really that hard?"

I looked down and realized I was still holding Rudy's empty glasses. I rolled my eyes and handed them to a passing waiter. "Have you ever had the misfortune of meeting Rudy Malkin?"

Lizzy let out a flabbergasted sigh. "Cripes, he isn't here, is he? I can't stand that guy."

"You know him then?"

"Me and every other magical person on the island. I know you think I'm a troublemaker, but Rudy is on a whole different level. I thought he was still in prison."

"Prison? What did he do?"

"Gosh, what didn't he do? I think he's ticking off every crime he possibly can. He loves to wreak havoc wherever he goes. The last I heard his ex-girlfriend bought a car for her new boyfriend, and Rudy set fire to it."

"What a charmer."

"Yeah, he's a wildcard all right." Lizzy looked up at the churning sea picture. "Ooh, I like this one."

"Rudy claimed he's the artist behind it," I said.

Lizzy laughed. "Rudy? Oh, I'm sure. I bet he told you all sorts of things. Here's a handy tip: If his mouth is open, he's lying."

"Seems like an odd thing to lie about, he said he has a meeting with Zaza."

"Poor Zaza," Lizzy laughed to herself. "Speaking of which, he's unveiling his 'Grand Masterpiece' in about ten minutes. There's one more exhibit to display on stage. We can go after that."

"Good," I said. "Maybe I can get some much-needed sleep before we go and spring Adam from this werewolf jail, or whatever it is that's going on." I found myself looking up at the stormy scene again. "What do you think this means?"

"I don't know," Lizzy shrugged. "The sea is awesome?"

"Why do I talk to you?"

"Because you don't have any other friends!" she beamed. "Let's get another one of these bubbly orange things and head into the main room for this announcement."

Lizzy and I both waited in line for the bar—like civilized people—and made our way into the main room after we got our drinks, where the majority of the crowd now waited in front of a stage.

Zaza's pint-sized assistant, Poppy, was currently waiting on the stage, cue cards in one hand and a drink in the other. She was a tiny figure of a woman, swamped in a cherry-blossom pink cardigan which was accented by big chunky eyeglasses. Her dark black hair fell at her shoulders, cut sharp and shiny as glass.

I imagined I would see her picture if I looked up 'nervous' in the dictionary.

"When's Zaza coming?" I asked Lizzy as I checked my watch once again. "Not that I'm not enjoying all this culture, but I really want to get a nap in before our midnight exhibit."

"You know what these celebrities are like," Lizzy said. "Anything to build suspense."

Just then Zaza's bodyguard Scott walked onto the stage, pulling a flatbed trolley, upon which there was a huge wooden crate. He wheeled it to the stage's center, whispered something to Poppy and then hurried off the stage.

An excited hush whispered through the crowd and the ever-nervous Poppy approached a microphone stand at the stage's front. She cleared her throat.

"It seems Zaza has retired for the night," she said. "But in his absence, he has asked me to present his final piece for this exhibit, a piece that he hand-crafted himself from Tasmanian Emerald over the course of nine months. Here is a brief message from Zaza himself." Poppy held up the cue cards. "Keys. They are portals to other worlds. They open doors. They lock away secrets. These small and innocuous objects construct a framework of boundaries on which our deepest desires and greatest fears reside. With them, we can hide our most terrible lies, without them, would we ever rest at night?"

Poppy lowered the cards and held her hands behind her back. She nodded at someone standing behind the curtains and Zaza's herculean bodyguard came back onto the stage, with a crowbar in his hand. He wedged the flat end into the front of the crate and pulled it open. As the panel loosened Poppy addressed the crowd one more time.

"Presenting *The Omega Key*. The most intricate emerald sculpture in the world!"

The crowd already began to clap, but they stopped when Zaza's musclebound guard pulled the loosened panel aside, revealing the contents within the crate. The applause stopped abruptly, cries sweeping across the room as we all saw what lay within.

There was no emerald sculpture inside.

Slumped inside the box was the unmistakable body of Zaza LaFoo. His signature black shades were missing, his eyes rolled back and his tongue lolling from his open mouth. The grey pallor of his skin and crumpled up body were sign enough that he was dead. The blunt wound on his head and dried blood running down his face were sign all the more.

"Is this some pretentious artistic stunt?" Lizzy whispered to me.

"I don't know Lizzy, but I know one thing for sure. There's a dead guy in that box."

4

"It's one heck of a way to end a show, I have to give Zaza that," I said to Lizzy.

"He might have a hard time repeating this one at future exhibits," she added.

"I can only agree with you there."

We were standing outside the museum after being escorted outside by the staff. Some of the guests had gone home now, but most were hanging around out of sheer nosiness. I was waiting to see Deacon. It would only be a minute or two until the police arrived, and he'd been dodging my calls all day. I appreciated that he might want a bit of space and time to think, but if I could just talk to him and explain, I might be able to make things right again.

Several cruisers pulled up and I scanned the police for sign of Deacon, my heart sinking as I didn't see him. I did see two familiar faces however, Mark and Clark Stark, two of Deacon's deputies.

"Mark, Clark!" I shouted, catching the attention of the twin officers before they ducked into the museum.

Mark and Clark were both identical twins. They each had spiky black hair and strong glasses prescriptions. Both turned at once, saw me in the crowd and smiled. To my relief they came over.

"Oh, Chelsea! Fancy seeing you here! You trying to get another case under your belt?" Mark asked.

"Probably tuned into the police frequency!" Clark joked. They both laughed.

"Very funny," I said. "I happened to be inside when they found the body. I'm not here for any mystery solving. I was waiting to see Deacon. Is he around?"

"Ah, afraid not," Clark said. "He's gone up to Delfino on an elective training week."

"Elective training week?" I asked.

"Yes," Stark answered. "We all have to go up there every couple of years for some training. Deacon technically doesn't have to go now, but he called the station this morning and said he'd booked it in. I dare say he just wanted some time on the beach!"

"Yeah, probably," I said. "Thanks guys."

Mark and Clark both nodded cheerily and ducked under the police tape that their colleagues were setting up around the museum.

"Come on," I said to Lizzy as I hurried her away from the front of the museum. "If we're quick I can get an hour in before we have to fight werewolves in the woods."

"Don't you want to stay here and snoop around a crime scene?" she said. "Break in and look for clues? Butter up the Stark brothers and get on the other side of the police tape?"

"No, I want sleep! And make sure you don't drive like a maniac on the way back!"

Ten hectic minutes later Lizzy skidded onto the front driveway of my house. I quickly got out of her giant black SUV and reminded myself that I really needed to sort out my own ride now I had a bit of money. Lizzy was something of a frightening driver, most of the women in my family were actually. I was starting to wonder if I was the only one without a death wish.

"What can I do while you're napping? Can I raid your fridge?" Lizzy asked as we hopped up the stairs to the front porch.

"Artemis already ate all the ice cream, but go nuts. I—"

The front door swung open just as I went to put my key in,

revealing an enthusiastic looking Selena, accompanied by my resident pirate ghost Old Mad John.

"Welcome to Chateau Sponks!" Selena sang ceremoniously. "Where you can tell all your problems to…" She looked over at the floating pirate ghost and nodding encouragingly.

"Get out!" he said, smiling from ear to ear with both arms held out.

"Not bad, timing could use a little work though," I said as I walked in. "Selena this is my cousin, Lizzy. Lizzy this is Selena, aka the Pendle Puma. Yada, yada. Why don't you both have a cup of tea while I get some sle—"

"Chelsea you'll be delighted to know that I have taken care of all the garden work!" Selena said enthusiastically. Before I could protest, she hooked her arm around mine and escorted me through to the back garden. On the way through the kitchen I couldn't help noticing that every pot, pan, and utensil in my possession was out. Multiple pots were bubbling over on the hob, several casserole dishes were in the oven and the sink was full of washing up.

"Have you been cooking—" I said, trying to look over my shoulder to figure out what was going on.

"In a minute, garden first!" she said, ushering me outside.

There was a pretty big lawn behind the house and Adam usually took care of all the mowing. Currently I hadn't had to mow the lawn once, which was a good thing because lawnmowers didn't get on very well with me. I'm not sure why, but I always ended up churning up the turf and making a right mess of things.

Adam wasn't a wizard, but he certainly had a magical way with lawnmowers because the lawn always looked amazing when he was done, like a pristine blanket of billowy soft grass. Judging from Selena's efforts I would have done a better job myself.

"Uh… where's all the grass?" Lizzy asked.

"Ah good," I said, "I'm not the only one staring at a field of dirt."

"Well here's the thing," Selena said. "I've not used one of those ride on mowers before, and I think I put it on the wrong setting. I did one entire lap of the perimeter before I realized what had happened."

"And you then decided to scalp the rest of the lawn?" I said, trying to wrap my head around it.

"I figured it might as well all match. And it's symbolic if you think about it in a way. A new start," she said, one hand on my shoulder and the other in the air like she had just said something profound.

"Are you involved in some grass-seed MLM that I should know about?"

Selena laughed. "Not anymore! Worry not. Now we've got the garden out of the way I can show you what else I've been up to."

Walking back into the house I saw Artemis, who was sitting on one of the flowerbeds. "Oh, you're going to love this," he smiled. "Selena has been *really* helpful today."

Back inside I got to see the bombsite that used to be my kitchen.

"So, I didn't know what your favorite meal was, so I tried to make all the classics! We have lasagna, burgers, chili, pizza, curry, Mexican, Italian! All homemade!"

"And all burned!" Artemis announced proudly.

Selena laughed. "Only a little bit. It's a bit hard juggling ten meals at the same time, while trying to scalp the lawn! Mow. I mean mow the lawn!"

"Scalp does seem more accurate," Lizzy commented.

"You did all this at the same time? ...Why?!"

"Well I didn't have much time between coats of paint. That paint dried fast!"

"What paint?" I asked.

"I. Am. Such. A. Klutz!" Selena said. "I completely forgot to mention!" Once again, the lanky brunette pulled me out of the kitchen and back into the hallway, pointing admirably at the wall running up the stairs. "I figured you could use a fresh coat of paint on the hallway, so I did a couple of quick coats!"

"Did you..." Lizzy said as she leaned into inspect the fine handy-work. "Did you paint over the picture frames?"

Selena laughed nervously. "Yes, that wasn't part of the plan in the beginning. I thought I could save time by painting around the frames, but then I got a spec of paint on one and well, you know, I couldn't just leave it at that!"

"So you decided to paint over *all* of my picture frames?" I said, my brow knotting so tight with confusion that I thought I was going to trigger a snap migraine.

"I figured it could be a fun little game. Do you ever find yourself walking up the stairs and wish you had something to do?"

"All the time," Artemis said. He was being sarcastic of course, but I was starting to realize Selena might not pick up on things like that.

"Well now you do!" she said and pulled out a coin. "Now you can stop every now and then and scratch away a bit of the paint, revealing a fun picture of your loved ones! I was going to paint the rest of the house so I can do the other frames—"

"No!" I said quickly. "No, I mean, there's just… paint's so expensive it's probably best we leave it at one wall for now." I turned and looked at Lizzy. "Quick question. Is there such a thing as *Candid Camera* but for witches?"

"Nope," she said, smiling at the chaos of the current situation.

"So this is all happening for real," I said to myself in grim realization.

"Oh dear," Selena said, perhaps finally cottoning on that she was the complete antithesis of the word helpful. "None of this is useful, is it? I'm afraid I might still have a bit of brain fog left over from shifting back. It takes a bit of time to adjust, especially after spending a long time in one form. Puma minds and human minds are quite different."

"I'm starting to see that," I said, taking a very deep breath to try and center my thoughts. I wasn't really bothered about any of this. I knew that Selena was just trying to help, I'd just made the mistake of taking in a lodger that was absolutely bonkers. "But look, nothing here can't be fixed, and we have magic on our side too. Maybe just… ask first before making any further changes. As I said before you're welcome to stay here and just relax. You don't have to do any of these jobs."

"Even though you do them so well," Artemis said. I shot the cat a look and he closed his mouth.

"The most helpful thing you can do is help me out with this Adam thing. You know where this pack is, right? Lizzy said she'd drive us over later. Now if you don't mind, I need to get a little sleep before midnight, otherwise I'm going to drop dead on my feet."

If I could even sleep at this point. My entire house was basically upside down, my boyfriend had run off to literally bury his head in the sand and *another* body had turned up on the island.

"Of course," Selena said, looking very sympathetic to my cause. "You have an hour of peace and quiet, but—oh."

"Oh?" Lizzy asked.

Oh? I didn't like the sound of that. I mustered my best smile and braced myself for whatever was coming next. "Oh?"

"Well it's just…" she said, wringing her hands over one another like she was drying an invisible shirt. "The mattress might still be a little wet. It's not had much time to dry."

"Wet?" I said, smiling through my teeth. "Why would it be wet?"

"I gave it a hose down in the shower, to clean it. Now that I hear myself say it out loud, I realize that was an incredibly stupid thing to do." She tapped her head, crossed her eyes and laughed to herself. "Doy! Sorry. Puma brain strikes again. I promise I will be normal soon."

"That's… that's fine," I said, trying my very best not to breakdown right there and cry. "I will just go and sleep on the spare bed in the basement. It's just for a nap."

"Great!" Selena said. "Lizzy, perhaps you can help me pop all the windows out of the frames while Chelsea sleeps. If we whack them in the dishwasher now, they'll be clean by the time she wakes up!"

Lizzy laughed nervously. "That's not how windows work. Um, why don't we just go and sit in the lounge and read quietly?" she said, putting a hand on Selena's shoulder and steering her away from whatever chaos she was headed for next. "You can tell me all about your time as the puma…"

I could only hope Lizzy would somehow contain storm Selena while I tried to grab forty winks on the creaky spare bed in the basement. I made my way back into the kitchen, kept my eyes fixed firmly on the floor to avoid the mess and unlocked the basement door and shut it behind me.

A small voice on the stairs scared the life out of me.

"Want me to give you a small charm? It'll help you rest up."

"Artemis!" I screamed. He must have snuck through the door with me right before I shut it. I pulled the dusty old string that turned on the stairwell light and walked on down. "Do I need to put a bell on your collar?"

"Sorry," he said. "I thought you'd want some company. You seem a little stressed out and I thought I could help calm you down."

The basement was actually surprisingly big, it's floor plan partially extending past the boundaries of the house. It felt small at the moment because it was still full of years of my Great Aunt Griselda's clutter. Since inheriting her house, I hadn't had a chance to clear any of it out yet. It looked a little spooky down here and I didn't like it generally, but I was so tired I didn't care.

I tip-toed around the mounds of old junk and collapsed onto the old bed in the far corner. Rusted springs wheezed as the lumpy mattress sagged under my weight, and plumes of dust filled the air. Something hard and sharp dug into my back. I shifted my weight around until I found a spot on the mattress where I could almost forget about the sensation of being jabbed in the back by rusted metal.

"Just great," I said, staring up at the grim ceiling.

"If it's any consolation I did try and stop her, but I'm just a small cat."

"It's okay, none of this is your fault. I just can't understand any of this. She's acting like a crazy person."

"This is all expected behavior," Artemis said, jumping up on the bed to curl up at my side.

"In what universe is this expected behavior?" I asked, shifting on the bed again. "What is wrong with this mattress? It feels like the statue of liberty is hidden underneath this thing!"

"Calm down princess. Selena has been in her puma form for… Avalon knows how long! Years maybe? Even a shifter like her should switch back more regularly. She's just going through phases of shift-sickness, a normal process whenever a shifter switches over to another form after a long time. It happened to me when they turned me into a familiar for the first time."

"It did?" I asked.

"Oh yeah," he nodded. "I'm still a human technically, but a cat mind and a human mind are very different things. All of your thoughts are completely upside down, it takes a few days to settle and be yourself again. My first week as a familiar I put all of Griselda's boots in the fire because I thought it would help warm them up."

I laughed. "I bet she loved that."

"She was furious! She was on the phone to the familiar academy, howling that I was defective, and she was going to send me back! They didn't really explain this sort of thing back then, just dumped cats with witches and let them figure out all the mess. I hid on the roof for a week until she calmed down. Anyway, I digress. Want a little sleep charm? I can help you have a good rest before we have to go rescue the moron."

"No charms," I said, my eyes already drooping despite the current unrest in my life. "Just talk about something boring. You're pretty good at that."

Artemis feigned a mock gasp. "How very dare you! But okay. Now that you mention it, I watched a great episode of *Hammered* earlier. Wanna hear about it?"

"Sure." *Hammered* was an over-the-top courtroom drama about a young female lawyer carving her way through the world of love, law, and litigation. I thought it was utterly insane, but Artemis loved it. "What's happening in the world of Molly Mox this week?"

"Oh boy! It's a doozy! Molly has a court case against the cartel, and she also has to find a lost piece of treasure with her submarine!"

"I thought she sold her submarine to pay off her brother's gambling debts?" I said sleepily. Molly was a lawyer, but deep-sea exploration was one of her many realistic hobbies.

"No, she got it back after she solved the piñata murders. So Molly is swamped at work, but she's just got a new secretary, and get this… he's a man! And handsome!"

"Wow, what a twist…" I said, my eyes closing one last time.

The next time I opened them again the world was delightfully silent. For a second anyway. I was lying in the exact same position and Artemis was sleeping next to me. The basement door opened, and I heard Lizzy shouting something to Selena.

"Let's just leave the lightbulbs all screwed in for now? Yeah. They don't need a rest!" She sighed, and then more gently, "Chelsea? You up? It's time to go and sort out this thing with Adam."

"I'm up. I'll meet you out front in five minutes."

I left Artemis sleeping on the bed and met Lizzy and Selena in the hallway upstairs. Lizzy was trying to wrestle a box of tea out of Selena's hands.

"Put the tea down Selena!" Lizzy said.

"But I need to staple them to the skirting boards! What if the mice need caffeine?!"

Lizzy snatched the box of teabags from Selena and looked at me in a way that said *dear god help.* "Chelsea! You're awake! Sleep well?"

"Like a rock. And by that, I mean it felt like I was sleeping on rocks." It was only a short nap, but it would be enough to keep me going for now. "You guys had a nice relaxing time?" Judging from the look on Lizzy's face this had been a fraught hour of trying to corral Selena's temporary lunacy.

"Let's just go," Lizzy said, placing the box of teabags on the hall floor. She hurried out through the front door to her car, glad to be free of babysitting duties for a little bit.

"Are we going somewhere?" Selena asked me.

"We need to help Adam, remember?" I said. The reminder seemed to sober her up a little.

"Adam! I completely forgot. Come on Chelsea, we'll have to staple the teabags later, there's no time for that right now."

"Well darn," I said, snapping my fingers as Selena hurried out the door after Lizzy. A few minutes later we were on the road, Lizzy's SUV racing over the winding forest roads of Pendle Island. Selena gave directions along the way. Now that she had an actual task at the forefront of her mind, she appeared to be a little more focused.

"So the gate is just down here on the right," Selena said. "The pack have a small settlement on the other side. It's protected by magic, so it looks like an empty field most of the time, but there's a few minutes every midnight where they can grant access to folk outside the pack."

"I've never actually met a werewolf," I said, "apart from Adam anyway. Are they dangerous?"

"Distrusting, I'd say. Very cagey. You have to be careful what you say around them. Don't mention vampires for example, they hate vampires. We'll have to leave the car outside too."

Lizzy pulled up at the gate and we all climbed out. I found myself staring at sparse woodland and an empty and open field. The night was unusually quiet. Suddenly a man appeared on the other side of the gate. He looked normal enough, but his eyes had an unusual yellow glow.

"Selena, you're in your human form. What are you doing here?"

"We've come to see—"

Selena's words were cut short by the howl of a loud motorbike, which screeched off the road and skidded right across the track in front of us, stopping us all in our tracks as we walked up to the gate. The rider turned off the engine and climbed off his bike.

"You!" I gasped, looking at Rudy Malkin. "What are you doing here?! Are you following me?!"

Rudy looked both confused and amused to see me. He had a large duffel bag over his shoulder. He stared at the man behind the gate, and then back at us. "You? I told you I'm not interested in joining your vampire cult, leave me alone!"

"I—what?" I said, left standing in confusion as Rudy approached the gate.

"I'm here to see Harper. Open up."

The yellow-eyed shifter glared at Rudy but opened the gate. Rudy stepped through and disappeared on the air. The shifter closed the gate again. "Take your vampire business and leave," he said, looking at Lizzy and me.

I couldn't believe that jerk Rudy was here to ruin my night again.

"We're not here about vampires!" I pleaded to the shifter at the gate. "I'm here to help Adam!"

"The thief," the shifter said dismissively. He looked at Selena. "This is the witch you wanted to bring?"

Selena nodded. "Yes, she'll help get your cup back."

"Chalice," he corrected. "But fine. You may enter. You have twenty minutes." We all advanced but he held up his hand and stopped Lizzy. "Stop right there. You can't come in."

"But I'm with them!"

He shook his head. "No, no vampires. Those are the rules."

Her mouth dropped open. "I'm not a vampire, I'm a punk!"

The shifter narrowed his eyes. "Still. Too pale. My kind don't like that. You wait out here."

Lizzy crossed her arms and huffed. "Fine. Whatever." She looked at us. "I'll wait in my car and listen to my vampire audiobook." She glared at the shifter. "I'll open the window so you can hear too!"

"Come," the shifter said, opening the gate for Selena and me, so we could walk through. We stepped through the gate and suddenly a small forest and a village of wooden huts appeared across the field. I couldn't help gasping, it took my breath away.

"Welcome to Laika," Selena said to me. "Pretty cool huh?"

"No whispering," the shifter said as he looked back us. "Follow me and stay close. You see Harper first."

"Harper?" I asked, but our escorting shifter took no notice of me.

"The alpha," Selena whispered. "He's the one in charge. He'll decide if we live or die." Her voice sounded a little too cheery for that particular sentence.

"Oh, great," I said, feigning my best smile.

What a wonderful evening this was turning out to be.

5

"*E*yes forward, stop talking and stay close."

"What crawled up your butt, wolf boy?" I said to the shifter escorting us through the hidden forest settlement.

"My name is Dean, and we're all under a lot of pressure at the moment. Tensions are high in Laika."

"Because of the cup thing?" Selena asked. "It's because of the cup thing, isn't it?"

"It's a chalice," Dean growled, "and yes, it's very important to us. Your friend doesn't realize how much trouble he's in, and perhaps you don't either."

We followed Dean along paths that twisted around the village's many log cabins. I had to admit this placed looked cute, and cozy too. "The village is nice," I said, trying to smooth things over with Dean a little. Pendle Island was already keeping me busy enough, I didn't need a pack of mad wolf shifters on top of that too.

"Thank you," Dean said.

"Middleclass suburbanites would pay top dollar to come and stay in a place like this for a weekend."

"We built Laika to get away from those types," Dean said, his yellow eyes glaring back at me as we hiked up a path covered in fallen pines. "And I told you to stop talking."

Charming.

A large cabin stood at the very back of the village. It looked like it functioned as the town hall. As we arrived Rudy came out through the tall front doors. He looked at me and rolled his eyes.

"You actually got in?" He looked at Dean. "Man, you guys just let anyone in these days."

"Stay here," Dean said to Selena and me. "I will tell Harper you have arrived." Dean disappeared inside, leaving us alone with Rudy.

"What are you doing here? And why do I get the feeling your following me?" I said to him.

He just laughed. "Um, first of all, that's none of your business, stop trying to stick your nose where it doesn't belong, and second of all, *you're* following me." He looked at Selena. "Who's this?"

"Selena," she said. "We went to Pendle High together. You were a few years above me."

"No chance, I'd remember a pretty face like yours. What do you say we get dinner together some time?"

"What happened to your elbow?" I said, fully wedging myself in the middle of Rudy's awful pickup attempt. I'd only just noticed, but a patch was missing from the elbow of his leatherjacket, and his elbow was bleeding.

"Huh?" Rudy twisted his arm around and saw the bleeding. "Oh. I came off my bike on the way over here. Must have scuffed my arm."

"What was in the bag?" I asked. "Do you have business with the wolf pack?"

He stared at me like I was dense. "What part of…. 'none of your business' don't you understand?"

I folded my arms; I wasn't going to budge this time. I didn't know what was going on with this character, but he was setting off all sorts of alarm bells. "You just seem calm considering the news."

"What news?" Rudy said. He was starting to look frustrated now. "Do you always talk in riddles?" He looked at Selena. "Is she always this annoying?"

"Zaza," I said. "You said you knew each other. I figured you'd be more upset about his death."

Rudy laughed, though it appeared to be more out of confusion. "What are you talking about?"

"Zaza," I repeated. "He's dead. Stuffed in a box, revealed as the final piece in his show. You didn't see that?"

"I didn't see the idiot all night. I had to get my money from his assistant Poppy. I'd been waiting long enough."

"Money?"

"For the work. Most of the pieces in that exhibit are made by me. Zaza's a Warhol type, he's just the image while other artists do the work anonymously. He has a whole collective of people behind the scenes. It's a joke with no punchline really. I do all the work and then he pays me less than he agreed, months after he was meant to."

"Sounds like a good motive to kill him."

"I told you, I didn't see him. I got the money and left. I—" Rudy stopped himself. "Hold on one second, I just remembered that none of this is your business. I see what you're doing here, the annoying detective thing? Do it somewhere else. I didn't kill that jackass, and I only talked to two people at that show: you and Poppy." He lifted a hand and pointed at me. "Follow me again and we have problems."

He walked past me, his boots crunching over the dirt as he made to leave.

"I didn't follow you!" I said. "I have stuff to do here!"

"Don't care, leave me alone!" Rudy shouted without looking back.

Dean came out. "Harper will see you. Hurry."

Selena and I went inside. He led us down the hallway to a workshop, where a huge man with short black hair was working a bandsaw. He stopped when he saw us come in. I knew at once this had to be Harper, 'the alpha.'

He was a giant of a man with hard eyes and a strong face. His arms and hands were huge, and there was an intimidating air about him.

"Ah, Selena. And you must be the witch friend, Chelsea," he said, brushing sawdust off his hands as he came over to welcome us. I took his hand and expected my fingers to get crushed to dust, but he was gentle. He towered over the both of us. "My name is Harper. Welcome to my pack. Dean, you may leave."

Dean nodded and left the room.

"I was expecting a colder welcome," I said as Harper went back to his bandsaw. "I don't get the impression we're seen as friends of your people."

"Let's cut to the chase, shall we?" he said. "Your friend Adam has taken something from my people, a very valuable chalice. It's been in this pack for centuries and is a powerful werewolf artefact. It's said to be the same chalice from which Gilgamesh drank the cursed blood, the same blood that made him the first werewolf."

I blinked a few times as I absorbed the information. I knew nothing of werewolves or their origin, but if what Harper was saying was true then this wasn't just some ordinary cup.

"Okay…" I said, realizing that perhaps this was more serious than I initially thought. "Do you have proof it was him?"

"Yes. Several of my pack saw him leave with it."

"But…" But why? I just couldn't wrap my head around it. Why would Adam do something like this? He wasn't a thief.

"There are no two ways about it, Chelsea Sponks. He took the chalice, and we need it back for a very important ceremony. Until it's returned, he will remain a prisoner here. I cannot go back on that."

"All right. Could I talk with him maybe? Perhaps we can figure this all out. It's probably just one big misunderstanding."

"I hope you're right," Harper said. "Follow me. I can lead you to him."

Selena and I followed Harper out of the workshop and down a set of stairs, entering some sort of underground cells. There were four on each side of the corridor, all empty apart from the last one on the right. A pretty girl with long white hair stood on the outside of the cell, she was talking and laughing.

"Melody," Harper growled. "What did I tell you about talking to the prisoner?"

Melody immediately straightened up and dropped her smile. "Sorry Harper," she said. "I was just doing the rounds."

"Go and help the others get ready for the hunt. The prisoner has visitors."

The white-haired girl skipped past us and ran up the stairs. I looked into the cell and saw Adam.

"Chelsea!" he beamed. "You came!"

"I heard you were in trouble, so I came. That's what friends are for."

"I have explained the reason for your imprisonment," Harper said to Adam. "Your friend is here to help reclaim what you have taken." He turned and looked at me. "I will leave you to talk in private. You can find me in the workshop. Please come and see me before you leave."

"Thanks, will do," I said. Harper nodded and walked along the corridor and up the stairs, leaving the three of us alone. Adam was smiling from ear to ear, for someone that was in mortal danger, he seemed pretty happy.

In fact, I didn't recall ever seeing Adam like this. He was an outdoorsy type that kept his cards close to his chest. He was not... this.

"Selena! I'm so glad you found Chelsea, thanks for helping me out."

"No problem," she said. "Why don't you tell Chelsea what's going on?"

"That was Melody," he said to me. "The girl with the white hair? She's so beautiful. Isn't she great?"

"Seemed like Harper didn't want her talking to you."

"Oh? Yeah." He laughed. "He's her older brother. I guess he would be protective of her. She's just been so swell the entire time I've been here. She comes and visits every day, and we talk so much."

"I think she's your guard, Adam," I said. "I think she has to visit every day."

"Well yeah, but there's more to it than that."

Selena and I looked at one another. "Adam, Harper and his people think you stole their chalice. They're being relatively friendly now, but I don't think you realize how serious this is."

"Oh, I get it," he said. "The chalice is a pretty big deal, but they don't need it back just yet. I'm biding my time."

I blinked. "Wait, so you admit you stole it?"

"Huh? Oh yeah. I took it Chelsea," Adam's brow creased, and he laughed, looking at Selena like I was crazy for even having to ask. "No one's doubting that."

"So why did you ask me to come here and help you? Do you want me to get the chalice for you?"

"What?" Adam laughed again. "What? No. Look, you're not getting this at all. I took the chalice on purpose. It's all part of my master plan. You saw Melody, right? You saw how beautiful she is? I've been in love with her for ages. Well, I knew if I took the chalice Harper would lock me up. It meant I could be here more and see Melody every day. It's perfect when you think about it."

"Is it?" I asked, my voice straining high as I tried to find an iota of logic. Even Selena looked disturbed, and she was going through her brain fog shifter sickness.

"It's perfect. They want the chalice back; I know where it is. Until then I get to spend every day with Melody. And here's the real kicker, this is the part where I need help."

"Okay…"

"I'm only going to give the chalice back once Harper gives me permission to marry his sister. Now I've not mentioned that to either of them yet, because I'm still thinking of the right way to ask her, but now you know the whole story you have to agree, it's pretty good, right?"

I forced a smile and looked at my friend, who was out of his mind by all accounts. "Tell you what Adam, why don't you sit tight here, and I'll go and think up some creative ways to solve this conundrum."

He clapped his hands together excitedly. "I knew it was smart to get you in on this, Chelsea! Just wait until Melody hears about this!"

Selena and I left, heading back upstairs to find Harper back in the workshop. He stopped what he was doing and came over to us.

"You see the problem?" he asked.

"He's out of his mind," I said. "That's not Adam."

"I'm glad you noticed. He's not the only one. Melody, my younger sister, she is acting strangely also. Adam is not a stranger to this pack; we have crossed paths during his time on the island. He is neither a friend or foe, but he and Melody have grown close recently. You understand the bigger problem at task here, it's not just about the chalice."

"You want me to figure out why they're both acting so strange," I asked.

He nodded. "And return the chalice." He pulled a ring from his pocket and handed it to me. "This ring will grant you access to the village whenever you like. You are welcome amongst my people while you help us through this crisis."

"Adam isn't the one that brought me here, it's you," I said in realization.

"That's right," Harper said. "I suggested it to him, knowing full well he would take the idea up. I've read about you. It seems you have a mind for solving mysteries, well, I'm asking you for help with this one. Something has invaded my pack. I want it rooting out."

"I'm not sure I'm the person for this job," I said. Not only did I know nothing about werewolves, but I had no clue where to start with this one.

"I think you are," Harper said. "And you have lots of motivation to get the job done."

"I do?" I asked.

"Yes," he affirmed. "Adam is your friend, and he took something important from us. If we don't get it back soon, I will have no choice but to repay my pack in kind. They're already calling out for it. I can only control them for so long."

I shook my head. "What? What do they want?"

"His head," Harper said flatly. "Good luck Miss Sponks."

6

I didn't stick around at the camp long after that. Harper seemed cool and collected on the surface, but something in those yellow wolf eyes hinted at violence and rage. His threat against Adam had me spooked to say the least, and I didn't waste any time getting out of there.

When we finally got back to my house it was almost two in the morning. Selena thankfully went up to the guest room to sleep straight away, and Lizzy was so tired she decided to crash at my house too.

"I'll take the bed in the basement," I said. "You can crash on the couch."

"Stop being ridiculous, come on. We're witches. Let's act like it."

"Meaning?"

My cousin sighed and pulled me by the arm, leading me into the lounge. "Stand by the fireplace and hold your hands out. Think of a nice four poster bed. And focus."

"I can't summon a bed!" I said. I was still very early on in my witch training and I could just about manage basic food items at the moment.

"I'll do it. I've barely used any magic today any way, I've got a fair chunk of energy left in my tank. I need you to keep your hands open and focus on a word in your head: *Patentibus*."

"What does that mean?"

"It basically opens up your magic reserves and lets me tap into them. Summoning a bed is a fairly big thing, so I'll use both our magic."

I did as Lizzy said and held my hands out, repeating the word in my head over and over again. Lizzy stood on the opposite side of the room and muttered a short spell under her breath, suddenly a giant four poster bed appeared a foot off the ground and dropped to the floor with a crash.

"Oops," Lizzy chuckled. "A bit high. But… ta-da! One cozy bed. Mind if we top and tail? I don't have it in me to summon another one."

"As long as you don't snore or kick my head," I said. I climbed right into the bed, not even bothering to change out of my clothes. My nap earlier had helped a little, but I was ready to sleep now for sure.

My head hit the pillow and my eyes started to droop right away. The bed felt great, and I was ready for a nice long sleep.

Little did I know, Artemis had other plans.

"I'm dying! Help me, I'm dying!" a distant voice wailed, stirring me from the depths of slumber. I opened my tired eyes and squinted at the clock on the mantlepiece. It was just after six in the morning.

Groan.

"Nurse!" came the voice again. I recognized it as Artemis this time. "Nurse! Help me!"

Lizzy groaned awake at the foot of the bed, she opened her eyes and scowled at me.

"Is that Artemis?" she yawned. "What time is it?"

"It's time to get up, summon a catapult and fire that kitty to the other side of this island," I hissed. "We're in the lounge Artemis!" I shouted. "Come in here!"

"Woe is me!" he said, wailing from somewhere in the kitchen. "You have to help me!" His voice got steadily closer and he limped through the lounge door, he stopped upon seeing the bed. "Ooh, this is new! Are we having a sleepover?!"

"People get to sleep at sleepovers," Lizzy growled from under the covers.

"Are you sick, or magically cured?" I asked. Artemis seemed to remember he was supposed to be ill and limped over to the bed before hopping up and sitting on me.

"You have to help me," he said, wheezing the words as if he was lying on his deathbed. "I have the sniffles. A cold!"

Lizzy and I stared long and hard at one another. "You woke us up because you have a runny nose?" I said. I think he could hear the hostile edge in my voice.

"Chelsea this is serious!"

"If you have a cold then why are you limping?" Lizzy asked. "And why are you making your voice all dry?"

"Well I need sympathy," he said.

"Artemis we're about five seconds away from mailing you to China," I said. "We talked about this; the mornings are for quiet time."

"But this is an emergency!" he said. "I can't have a cold, it's bad news!"

"Give it a few days and you'll get over it," I replied. "You're fine, you drama queen."

"Chelsea you're not getting it. This isn't a regular cold, when familiars get sick we—" A sneeze interrupted Artemis and the bed suddenly vanished from underneath us. The three of us hit the lounge floor, all crying out in surprise in the one second fall.

"Artemis!" Lizzy yelled. She looked like she was about to kill him.

"I'm sorry!" he said. "It's this cold, it's—"

Once again, another sneeze interrupted Artemis. This time six golden cages suddenly appeared around the room. Each one had a white parakeet inside, and they all started squawking immediately.

Lizzy jumped to her feet straight away, her lips moving quickly as she slashed her hands through the air, sending off blasts of magic to dispel the cages and birds. "Okay, I think we might actually have a problem," she said, taking a deep breath to focus herself. "It looks like Artemis has a case of the witchups."

"The witchups?" I asked.

"A magical cold. Nothing serious, but it can cause your magic to act weird. Sorry I shouted at you Artemis, I guess you were right for once."

"I told you!" he said, his voice sounding nasal and congested.

"Well what do we do?" I asked. "Is there a spell to fix it? Or a vet we can go and see?"

"Rose Pharmacy in town," Artemis said. "Rebecca will know what to do."

"That drugstore is a mortal place, Artemis, I doubt they'll have a cold remedy for cats with magical colds."

"Nah they're pretty good," Lizzy said to me. "Rebecca is a witch. She handles all the magic folk in town whenever we get sick. Her husband Paul handles the humans, and she deals with the magic stuff. If anyone can help you, it's her."

"I guess I'll go and get you some magical cat medicine then," I said to Artemis.

"And some quiche," he said in his best victim voice. "That will help me feel better. And that ice cream we talked about."

"Of course, your highness." I looked at Lizzy and rolled my eyes. "What do you say, can you drop me off at this drugstore before you head to work?"

"Buy me breakfast on the way and we have a deal," she said. "Also, I'm using your shower before we leave."

"Sure, but give it a good check over before you turn it on. There's no guarantee Selena hasn't stuffed the showerhead full of gravy granules."

"It's so relaxing staying over in this house," Lizzy said.

"Try living here!"

After Lizzy was finished in the shower I also washed and put on some clean clothes. It seemed that Selena's chaotic touch hadn't yet made it to the bathroom, so the shower was relatively stress-free, but I did notice all the fridge magnets were stuck on the inside of the bath. Selena had, for some reason, spelled out 'Toucan Motorbikes?' with my magnetic scrabble tiles.

We left the house not long after that, giving Selena strict instructions to take the day off and resist any urges to 'help' around the house. I'm not sure if she was finally coming out of her brain fog, or if the task of looking after a sick cat made her more focused, but she seemed a little less loopy today, so I hoped she was on the mend.

Lizzy drove us into town, and we stopped for a healthy breakfast of coffees and pastries. I think everyone on the island had a sweet tooth like me, because practically every business here ran some sort of pastry counter on the side. It was business decisions like that which led to me putting on ten pounds since moving here, not that I was complaining, I was always within walking distance of a freshly-baked snack.

This town wasn't all bad.

We usually grabbed breakfast together a few times a week and one of our favorite joints in town was *Madam Crème's*, a 'delightful' little French bakery right at the center of town. It was run by a dreary and philosophical French woman by the name of Sophia Crème. Her customer service was lacking, but her patisserie skills more than made up for it.

"Good morning, Sophia!" Lizzy beamed as we skipped through the door. "How are you on this fine and drizzly morning?!"

Lizzy was only ever this upbeat when we were on our way to Sophia's bakery.

"Existence is suffering, and hell is other people," Sophia said in her somber French accent. She really knew how to suck the fun out of a morning. "But I am delighted to see my two favorite customers. How are we this morning my darlings?"

"Tired," I said. "We need a weapons-grade amount of coffee and sugar. Stat."

"I think I have just the thing," Sophia said. "Take a seat at the window and I'll bring your order over."

We both made our way over to the window and sat down. Sophia's café was a little different than the rest. There was a display cabinet full of her morning bakes, but no menu. She brought you what she thought you needed, and she charged everyone a different amount. I had no idea how she was still in business, but I never once complained about the orders she brought over. She always got it exactly right.

"There you are," she said, coming over with our orders a few minutes later. "Two extra-large lattes, with an extra shot of espresso for both of you. Also, a cheese toasty for Elizabeth…"

"Yes! Just what I wanted!" Lizzy fist pumped the air.

"And a ham and cheese bagel for Miss Chelsea."

"Nailed it," I said. That was *exactly* what I wanted.

"We also have two slices of pecan pie, and a meatball sub for Chelsea."

"No sub for me?" Lizzy complained.

Sophia contemplated the question. "No… your boss will bring in lunch. Chelsea won't have time. Enjoy! I'm going out back for a smoke. If anyone comes in, then tell them to ring the bell."

"She's a witch, she has to be," I said to Lizzy as we began to devour our breakfast.

"Nah, I used to think so myself, she's just really good at her job. Ha! Looks like you're picking up the bill today," she said, pushing the receipt over to me.

"Huh?" I said, my words muffled around a mouthful of bagel. I looked down at the bill, which was itemized and handwritten by Sophia. At the bottom there was the total, accompanied by a note: *'$34 and Chelsea pays.'*

What?!

Sophia came back in as we were getting ready to leave. I went to the counter to pay, putting down two twenties to cover the bill. "Keep the change Sophia, the food was especially brilliant today."

"I thank you darling, but I'm afraid I can only take the exact amount I asked for." She handed the six dollars back to me. This wasn't new. Lizzy and I were constantly trying to tip Sophia, especially as her made up prices always seemed a little on the low side. We usually just put the extra in the charity box on the counter. I went to do so and noticed it was missing.

"Uh, I guess I'll just keep the change then," I said.

"It's that thief," she said, looking at the empty spot where the small plastic charity box usually was. "You know the one. Swiped mine the other day. Scoundrel. I told you, hell is other people."

I had read something in the Pendle Piper about a string of charity box robberies. Deacon and his boys had yet to find a culprit.

Deacon.

Bang. The thought of my boyfriend came smashing through my chest like a wrecking ball, leaving an ache and a wave of anxiety that felt like it wouldn't shift for the rest of the day. Sophia must have read something on my face. She pulled a macaroon from the glass cabinet and put it into my hand. "Take this one for the road. You need it. Bye!"

Back outside I said goodbye to Lizzy, making plans to get dinner later once she was done with work. The tires of her oversized SUV squealed on the tarmac and she burst down the road and around the corner. I sent a silent prayer up to the witchy gods, asking them to look over all the unfortunate souls sharing the road with my cousin today.

Rose Pharmacy wasn't far from the bakery, and after walking a few blocks south I found myself in the right place. I'd only actually been to the drug store once since moving to the island, and that was only to pick up some aspirin. It was one street back from the main street in Pendle town, so I didn't cross it often.

Rain showers were frequent enough on the island that I quickly learned to always carry a raincoat in my bag, and this morning was no exception. My trusty anorak and umbrella kept me dry enough for the most part, and by the time I got to the drug store the sky was beginning to clear up anyway.

The bell on the door rang as I stepped inside. There was only one other customer in the store at the moment, a short fat man stood at the counter, seemingly arguing with the pharmacist on the other side.

"I already told you I'm fine!" he barked. "Just pack up the gauze and alcohol. And tweezers! I'll fix it myself."

"Mr. Wood I really insist that you take yourself to the emergency room—"

'Mr. Wood' snatched his bag of things from the pharmacist and slapped his cash down on the counter. "I don't have time for this. Thanks for nothing!"

I stepped to the side and watched as the grumpy short man shuffled his way to the front door. It looked like he had been hobbled. He only saw me at the last moment and suddenly looked surprised. "Pardon me," he mumbled, opening the door and leaving the store as quickly as he could.

"Do the rest of the seven dwarfs know that grumpy is in here?" I said, mostly speaking out loud to myself. The pharmacist chuckled and I walked towards the counter.

"Oh, he's always like that. He needs to see a doctor straight away, but he's stubborn. Thinks he can do it all himself. There's only so much I can do. Anyway, I do believe you're new around here, my name is Paul Rose, my wife and I run this store. How may I help?"

"Chelsea Sponks," I said. "My cat—" I stopped myself, remembering exactly why I had come in here. I didn't exactly know how to broach this; all I knew is that I needed to speak to 'Rebecca' for magical queries.

"Is uh Rebecca in here? It's a... girl problem."

"Ah, say no more." The man turned around and looked into the back of the dispensary. "Rebecca, we have a young witch here needing your assistance!" I froze suddenly and he looked back at me, smiling. "Don't worry. The store is empty, and I know about all that stuff. Rebecca told me years ago when I asked her to marry me. It was quite a surprise at the time!"

My eyes widened at this opportunity. This man was basically Deacon from the future. I had to get his perspective while I could. It could help with Deacon.

"You weren't freaked out or anything? You didn't tell anyone else?"

"I thought she was crazy at first, and I still do, but that's nothing to do with magic." Paul chuckled to himself. "I guess after the initial shock it all seemed normal relatively fast, or as normal as these things can. I just accepted it. She was still Rebecca, still the woman I loved."

A woman suddenly appeared around the corner, stepping up to the counter to stand beside Paul. "I thought my ears were burning," she said. "Why are you buttering me up? What have you done?"

Paul shook his head and laughed. "You have a customer. Do your thing." He kissed his wife and went into the back. Rebecca looked at me, her face a picture of youthful intelligence.

"I know you!" she said delightedly. "The detective!"

"That's what it says on my birth certificate," I said. "Nice to meet you."

"Likewise. Maybe you can solve this one. What kind of lowlife steals a charity box?" Rebecca gestured to an empty spot on the counter. It looked like the drugstore had been hit too.

"I've been asking myself the same thing," I said. "But I'm also asking myself another question. Do you have anything to cure witchups?"

"For your familiar I take it?"

"Yes. One very dramatic cat."

Rebecca turned around and laughed as she scanned the shelves for something. "Oh, they're all like that. I've never met a familiar without a penchant for drama. My familiar, Luna, she's an absolute diva. Ah, here we are!"

She spun around on the spot and handed me a small bottle of shimmering purple liquid. There was a stopper on the top in the form of a copper skull.

"Looks… worrying," I said as she handed me the bottle.

"Just ignore the skull, it's part of the branding. It's Dr. Skull, he really is the best."

I turned the bottle around and looked at the label, which looked like it had been handwritten by a moody teenage vampire.

"Dr. Skull: Ravaging Remedies for Magical Maladies. Witchups Syrup, Birthday Cake Flavor," I said, reading the label out loud to myself. "Ooh, Birthday Cake flavor! …Artemis is not going to like that. Do you have chocolate fudge?"

"All sold out. …Artemis," Rebecca said to herself, teasing the name as she recalled something from the far flung reaches of her memory. "He was Griselda's familiar, wasn't he?"

"Yes, unfortunately I inherited him after Griselda died."

"More often than not Witchups are a reaction to something. If I recall last time, he got them after eating ice-cream. I believe he has some sort of magical allergy to the stuff."

"Ah… so the little devil knew."

"I beg your pardon?"

"Nothing, he's just been raiding the ice-cream extra hard lately."

"That explains it then! Have him take the syrup and avoid the ice-cream from now on, it will help minimize future Witchups episodes!"

"There's no instructions on here," I said. "Is it three teaspoons a day or something like that?"

"Nothing that complex! The skull is a little spritzer, see?" Rebecca leaned over and pushed the skull down. The little jaw opened, and a plume of purple smoke came out. A gravelly voice accompanied it.

"Dry flat hair? Try Dr. Skull's Bountiful Bounce Balm! Put the hurl back in your curls!" the bottle said.

"Quite the tagline," I said.

"Hey lady, I just read the lines!" the small copper skull said before going still again.

"Give Artemis a spritz of this at 1:11, 2:22, 3:33, 4:44 and 5:55," Rebecca said.

"Really straightforward," I said sarcastically.

"Oh honey, you should have seen the old remedy for the Witchups. Before Dr. Skull you would have to sing a Tibetan throat song for three whole days. Things are much easier now!"

"What a 'hashtag blessed life' I find myself in. It'll give Selena something to focus on at least. How much do I owe you?"

After paying Rebecca I thanked her for the prescription and headed back outside. The rain had stopped completely now, and the clouds had even cleared up a little. I took my jacket off as it was a little warmer than earlier, and put it into my bag. I started walking down the street back in the direction of the main street, deciding that I would get a little shopping done while I was in town. On a whim I pulled out my phone and tried Deacon again.

No answer.

"Come on Deacon," I sighed to myself and put my phone back in my bag. That's when I saw him again, not Deacon—Rudy Malkin.

I couldn't quite believe what I was seeing, but Rudy was across the street, slashing the tires of a car that was parked up on the side. There was no one else around at the moment so I was the only witness to this blatant daylight crime.

Enough was enough.

"You have to be kidding me!" I said. I tucked my bag under my arm and marched across the street to apprehend him. "Hey, bonehead!"

Rudy, who had just stabbed his knife into the last tire, shot his head up and looked at me. "Oh, you have got to be kidding me," he grumbled to himself, tucking his knife into a holster on his waist as he stood up straight to face me. "I have had enough Chelsea Sponks. This is blatant harassment! I told you to stop following me!"

"I was on my way out of the drugstore actually. And this is blatantly vandalism, what on earth do you think you're doing?"

"Not to sound like a broken record, but it's none of your—quick! Follow me!"

Rudy grabbed me by the hand and yanked me off the street, running away from the car and ducking down a side alley until we were both crouched behind a large dumpster.

"Get off me!" I said. "Let me go!"

"Shush!" he hissed. "You're going to ruin it!"

"Ruin wha—" I began. Rudy clamped a hand over my mouth, and I pushed it away. "Don't you touch me!"

"Well shut up then!"

A young girl came back to the car, no older than eighteen by the looks of it. She opened the trunk and threw something inside. She shut it again and then I heard police sirens. The girl looked startled, but there was no time to react. Two police cars suddenly pulled up right alongside the car and I saw Mark and Clark Stark get out.

"Where is he, miss?!" Mark shouted to the young girl.

"What?" the girl said, looking like she wanted to be anywhere else.

"We received report of a strange man attacking a young girl and her car, just five minutes ago, you said he slashed your tires!"

"No one slashed my tires—" she began.

"These tires have been slashed all right," Clark said as he rounded the car. "Come on, you can tell us. Which way did he go?"

"What the heck is going on here?" I whispered to Rudy.

"A genius is at work, that's what. Watch this."

Rudy pointed his finger at the trunk of the car and whispered something under his breath. The trunk suddenly popped out. The girl scrambled to close it, but Mark had already seen inside.

"Hang on a second," he said, forcing the trunk open again. "What in the mother of pearl is this? Clark, get a look!"

Clark came around and got a look too. The brothers looked at one another, their faces mutual pictures of amazement. "Care to tell us what these charity boxes are doing in the trunk of your car, miss?"

"I, I can explain!" she said.

"You can explain back at the station," Mark said. "Phone it in Clark. Looks like we caught the charity box bandit." He cuffed the girl and hoisted her into the back of the cop car.

"Wait a second," I said to Rudy. "You set this up? You helped them catch the box bandit."

"Why do you sound so surprised? I use my magic for good, even if my means are a little scrupulous."

"I'm just surprised is all," I said. "You're something of a suspicious character, you don't exactly make it easy to trust yo—" My words cut short as my phone started ringing in my pocket. Loudly.

"Turn it off!" Rudy hissed. I pulled out my phone and killed the call, but it was too late. Mark and Clark were already looking over in the direction of the alley.

"Is someone hiding there?" Mark Stark shouted.

"Come out with your hands up!" Clark added. They both walked forward with their guns out until they saw Rudy and me.

"Chelsea Sponks, and Rudy Malkin," Mark regarded. "Looks like Chelsea is already hot on the case! How did you find him?!"

"What? I can explain," I began. Where did I even begin?

"Stand aside Chelsea, you're good in our books. He's the one we want."

"Wait," Rudy said as Mark and Clark hoisted him up. They turned him around and cuffed him too. "What did I do?!"

"We've been looking for you all morning Malkin," Clark said. "Even paid a visit to your house, but you weren't in. Let's go down to the station and have a talk."

"About what?!"

"The murder of one Zaza LaFoo," Stark clarified. "We've got some questions to ask, and you're our lead suspect."

I watched, speechless, as Mark and Clark escorted Rudy into the front car. He turned back and looked at me, shouting across the street as they shoved him into the back.

"Chelsea, you have to help me on this! I didn't do it! I swear!"

The door slammed shut and I found myself helplessly lost, watching as the cruiser pulled away, leaving me standing in the alley-way, feeling somewhat dumbfounded.

The police had just taken Rudy in as their lead suspect, and with his last words to me he chose to proclaim his innocence. This entire morning had been bizarre from start to finish, but the oddest thing is that I couldn't get Rudy's words out of my head.

I think I believed him.

I had to help.

7

———————

*C*lark and I pulled up to the station. Mark had already arrived a few minutes earlier and he had taken Rudy inside. Clark climbed out of the car and I followed him.

"Look, can you tell me what's happening here?" I asked as Clark escorted the cuffed teenage thief. "Why is Rudy one of your main suspects?"

"Because of his track record, and he was one of the last people to speak with Zaza before he died."

"But Rudy said he didn't talk to Zaza."

Clark looked at me, practically rolling his eyes. "Quick tip with Rudy Malkin, Chelsea, if his mouth is open then—"

"He's lying, yeah, yeah, I've already been warned."

I followed Clark inside, and he stopped me at the reception. "Wait here and I'll get you a visitor's badge. I'll just give miss sticky hands here to one of the deputies for processing."

"Why do I need a visitor's badge?" I asked.

"Because you're helping of course. You helped us bring Malkin in!"

Clark disappeared down the corridor, leaving me at the reception with the lovely Barbara, a curly-haired she-devil with all the personality of a piece of paper. "Good morning Barbara," I said.

"Sherriff Long isn't here," she said flatly, her dull little eyes magnified behind huge spectacles last in fashion during the eighties.

Kind of retro though. I wish I had glasses like that.

"I'm aware," I said. "And where is he?"

"You don't know where your own boyfriend is?" she said with an assuming brow.

"Oh, I know, I just wanted to see if *you* knew."

"Sheriff Long is helping with administrative cover in Babonix," she said after a brief pause.

"Exactly. That's exactly what I heard."

Except the Stark brothers said Deacon was training in Delfino. *Liars, the lot of them!*

"Ah, Chelsea! There you are," Mark said as he remerged back in the hallway. He handed me a visitor's badge. "Couldn't have timed this better. Through here. She's this way."

She?

I followed Mark down the hall, and we turned into 'Interview Room 1' to find Verity Newport, Zaza LaFoo's trophy girlfriend. Mark closed the door behind us and joined Verity at the table. I was left standing in front of the closed door, looking around and feeling confused.

"Miss Newport this is Chelsea Sponks, an amateur investigator. She's helping us out on this case."

"I am?" I said.

Mark glanced back at me, looking as confused as I felt. "Yeah, didn't Clark go over this with you in the car?"

"No, he didn't. And why do you need my help?"

"Look Chelsea these things just go easier when you're involved. Let's skip past the protest and interview Miss Newport, shall we? You'll get paid for your time."

"Should I be worried?" Miss Newport said, speaking to the both of us. "Such a professional investigation unit. Your detective doesn't even know she's on the case."

"A minor hiccup," Mark said. He pushed out a chair and gestured to me. "Chelsea?"

I sighed and resigned myself to the hands of fate. I took a seat in the chair and gave Verity Newport a quick look over. There was no denying that she was pretty. She also had the accompanying vacuous stare one came to recognize with the ultra-attractive.

"What do you want to know?" she said to the two of us. I decided to hold my tongue, letting Mark take the lead.

"What's your favorite color?" he said after a moment of strong contemplation.

"Oh, for heaven's sake," I said, snatching the manilla police folder from his hands. I leaned forward and scanned the scant profile, closed the folder and threw it on the table. "Tell us about the night from your perspective."

"I was at the show. Zaza turned up dead. I went home and drank. Now I'm here."

"You went home?" I asked. "Straight away?"

"I needed to be alone. My boyfriend was murdered. That's quite the shock."

"When did you last talk to him?"

"Hm… that morning, in this sad little diner. We had an argument."

"About?"

"Oh, I don't remember. I think I was still mad at him over Gloria."

"Gloria?"

"This pathetic little girl from the country club. He was screwing around. Always was."

"Seems like a pretty strong motive for you to murder him."

Verity laughed. "Please. Zaza's been messing me around since day one. If I was the jealous type I would have killed him long ago."

"You don't seem too sad about his passing," I remarked.

"Of course I'm sad, but we were basically already broken up. We separated three months ago, I made it official."

"Why are you still hanging around with him then?"

"We're not really. It was just a paid gig for this weekend. He wanted me in the pictures for opening night. Said I made him look good. After that we were done for good. I'm going back to Tokyo. I'm doing a new film there. The next Godzilla? I'm in it. My agent says it's going to be huge."

"Godzilla usually is," I said without looking up at her. "All right Mark, I think we're good here."

"We are?" he said, a note of surprise in his voice.

"We are."

"But—"

"What's the suspected cause of death?" I asked Mark.

"Blunt force trauma to the head. The murder weapon is presumed to be the missing emerald sculpture."

"Any other clues?" I asked Mark.

"Glass on the floor from a broken window in a storeroom where Zaza's pieces were being held."

"So, we're looking at a robbery gone wrong, first guess. Take a look at Miss Newport, what do you see?"

"The girl from the gum commercials," Mark said.

"I—what?" I looked at him.

"Everest Gum!"

"Everest Gum," Verity repeated, pretending to pop a piece of gum into her mouth. She turned and winked. "Takes your breath to new heights."

"Did everyone on this planet forget how to write a good tagline?" I muttered to myself.

"I like it," Mark commented.

"I always thought it was pretty stupid," Verity said.

"That's great, but Mark, take a closer look at Miss Newport, what else do you see?"

He took a long hard look. I wasn't sure if he was actually taking anything in, or just enjoying this opportunity to stare at a pretty woman. "I… don't know," he said, finally giving in.

"No? Fine. I'll do all the work for you. Look at her nails."

"Nails?" he asked.

"Nails?" Verity turned them around so we could see. They were long, perfectly manicured, and flawless from top to bottom. "Romeo

Valancia. I have to go all the way to Italy to get them done, but he really is the best!"

"Fascinating," I said, "but Mark, take a closer look at her nails. Do you notice anything about them?"

He did indeed take a closer look, leaning forward like he was trying to read small print on a very important contract about life insurance. Once again, he sat back and gave a surrendering sigh. "They're very nice?"

"Oh, in the name of Madonna—they're flawless!" I said, spelling it out for him. "Not a break among them! Not a single chip, scratch, or fracture!"

"Ah… yeah," he said. "Very well looked after Miss Newport. Good job."

"Darling, you know nothing about female beauty regimes I see," Verity said.

"I'll have to admit I missed that lecture in cop college." Mark looked uncomfortable and out of place. Even Verity had clocked my line of thinking now. Mark wasn't going to get to the end by himself, so I decided to just give him the answer.

"Some cruel bugger smashed Zaza over the head with a paperweight Mark. Do you think Verity would be able to do that and keep those nails intact?"

Verity laughed out loud at the suggestion. "Not a chance!"

"Ah…" he said. "So… she's innocent!"

I wasn't sure I'd go that far yet, but I was pretty certain she wasn't the one to kill Zaza. "Most likely, but I think you should definitely stick around until this case is closed Miss Newport, you are a person of interest."

"Oh, but what about Godzilla?!" she said.

"I'm sure the production will survive without you. Now I already know the answer to this final question, but let me ask it anyway. Can you think of anyone that would have a good reason to kill Zaza?"

"Yes," she said. "Everyone."

"Why?"

"Because the man was an insidious moron."

"Jolly good. That'll be all." I looked at Mark and offered my best smile. "Are we done?"

"Yes, Mr. Hardy next. He's in Interview Room 2."

"Oh, I'm doing the whole kit and caboodle am I?"

"What's a caboodle?" he asked.

"Never mind, just hurry up so I can go home and give my cat his medicine."

<hr>

"Tell us about your position in Zaza's business, and give your perspective of the night's events," I said as we sat across the table from Zaza's head of security, Scott.

"I run security for Zaza, and act as his bodyguard. The night was normal enough until he turned up dead of course, I—" Scott had to stop himself, taking a moment to choke back tears.

If I didn't know any better, I'd say this was a strong reaction to a death, even for a bodyguard.

"Forgive me for saying this Mr. Hardy," I commented, "but you seem more affected by this death than I would have expected?"

"Affected?" he said, drying his eyes with the sleeve of his jumper. "Of course I'm affected, he was my brother!"

Both Mark and I looked at one another in surprise. *Well, that was a reveal and a half.*

"Brother?!" Mark said in shock. "But you look nothing alike!"

"Not all siblings are twins, Mark," I said, "believe it or not. But I do agree Scott, you are quite the opposite to one another."

"Keith had polio as a child. He ended up smaller than usual naturally. I've been looking after him most of my life, defending him from other kids and making sure he was all right. Even if I was his younger brother."

"Zaza's real name is Keith?" I asked. That was almost more surprising than them being related.

"Well it ain't frigging Zaza LaFoo, that was just a stage name. Just an image, like that ridiculous accent of his. He was born Keith, Keith

Hardy. My little older brother, gone, forever!" Scott broke out into another wave of hysterics. Mark offered him the tissue box, Scott blubbered a thanks and tried to compose himself.

"Look Scott," I said, "It seems that Zaza wasn't short of enemies. He was gifted at rubbing people the wrong way. I know he was your brother, and this is hard, but focus for a moment. All signs point to this being a robbery gone wrong. Did you uncover any sort of plot in the run up to this?"

"No," he said, taking a few calming breaths. "I run an airtight operation. Look, I can never forgive myself for this. I was supposed to protect Keith, and I failed. Now he's gone, gone forever, and it's all my fault."

"You can't be everywhere at once," I said. "You were watching the front door, just like he asked."

"But I let him in," Scott said.

"Him being?"

"That pit stain, Malkin! I don't know why we're sitting here talking if you have him. He's clearly the one to do it!"

So Scott suspected Rudy too?

"Why?" I said. "Why are you so sure it was him?"

"Just look at him!" he said. "He's a common crook. I warned Zaza about associating with types like that, but he would have none of it. Said he was too gifted an artist, needed his work for this show. If he was so gifted, then why didn't he just pay the man?!"

"Zaza didn't pay Rudy for his work?" I'd heard as much from Rudy. Was it possible that Rudy had killed him and took the emerald statue as reimbursement? Was that what was in the bag he gave to Harper at the shifter ranch?

"No, he was always ripping the artists off like that. The only thing Zaza liked more than fame was money. Once he had it, he didn't like to give it up, even if he'd made a promise! Just ask Poppy, Rudy had to get his money from her!"

"Poppy Chen?" Mark asked. "Zaza's assistant?"

Scott nodded. "She paid him out of her own pocket!"

"Rudy got his money then," I said. "So that would rule him out as a suspect."

The giant blubbering man just shook his head. "Nah. It wasn't about the money at that point. It was about making a point for that savage Malkin."

I looked at Mark, considering Scott's accusations. There was nothing else to talk about here. "I'm guessing we have Poppy Chen in Interview Room 3?"

"How did you guess?!"

"Let's just get this over with," I sighed as I pushed my chair back from the table.

"Magna Cum Laude, yes," Poppy said.

"Seems you are a woman of great distinction," I said. "So why work for Zaza?"

"Because he is a genius, the voice of a generation."

"A genius that doesn't pay the artists working for him."

Poppy twisted her lips. "I'll admit I never agreed with that. He had plenty of money, I don't know why he couldn't just pay people for their work. It was no secret that Zaza LaFoo was a collection of artists, he was the image. He gave them his vision, and they executed it."

"Rudy Malkin was one of these artists?"

She stilled at the mention of his name, even for just a second. "Yes. Look, I'm not stupid. I suppose you heard that I paid Rudy off."

"Would you like to tell us about that?"

Her cheeks were red, flustered at the line of conversation. "Zaza stiffed most everyone he worked with, but he didn't dare try it with me. I organized his entire business for him. Two people in his group always got their money, me and Scott."

"He paid you because the empire wouldn't run without your administrative expertise, and he paid Scott because he was his own brother."

"Exactly."

"But not the artists, and Rudy was no exception."

"Zaza really was a genius, but he was also a grinch. He suckered artists in with his name and big promises. He promised to pay an artist five times over their market rate and once the work was delivered, they never heard from him again."

"Why did other artists keep falling for this? If Zaza was a known raconteur?" Mark asked. I turned and looked at him with respect. That was actually a good question for Mark.

"Zaza is a smart as he is ruthless. He's a big name in the art world, he knows all the right people. His method was very simple. Use small time artists. Don't pay them. Threaten to blacklist them from the industry if they complain. He said the exposure was more than payment enough."

"Those delicious exposure bucks," I said. "I hear they go a long way."

"I didn't agree with it," Poppy said. "I already said that much. Zaza controlled one thing though, the money. I couldn't pay these artists even if I wanted to. I got him to pay a few people, but it was never even a fraction of what he promised."

"So why did you pay Rudy out of your own pocket?" I asked.

She looked down at the table for a second before answering. "Because he's an amazing artist," she said. "I don't know if you've seen much of the work in Zaza's latest exhibit, but you should check it out when you have a chance. Most of it is Rudy's, made under Zaza's name, and it's beautiful, some of the most breath-taking art I've ever seen."

"I was there on the night," I said. "I've seen the work; it is very good. How much did Zaza owe Rudy?"

"Close to one hundred thousand dollars. Rudy worked for months on those pieces."

"Where did you get that amount of money to pay him?"

Poppy laughed. "Zaza paid me well, but not that well. I gave Rudy most of what I had in savings. Close to thirty thousand."

I let out a long and slow whistle. "That's *very* generous. Did he know it was from you?"

"No, I lied and said that Zaza caved. I think a part of him knew."

"You must think Rudy an extraordinary artist if you're prepared to cough up that much dough," Mark said. A good steering point. Mark was getting better at this!

"It wasn't just about the art. Rudy is an exceptional individual. I know he has a past, and a lot of people judge him for it, but he's worth more than all of this. I can assure you he's not the one behind this senseless murder."

"Who is?" I asked.

Poppy shrugged. "I truly don't know, but I hope you tell me when you get to the bottom of it."

"I think we're done here," I said to Mark.

"One last thing actually. Why did you post Rudy's bail?"

That one threw me completely off guard. "What?"

Poppy looked at us both, her eyes flitting across the table. "Well he's innocent. That's why."

"Bail?" I said. "You're formally accusing him of this murder?"

"No, the tires. He slashed them on the car of that teenage girl. He confessed as much."

"The thief he helped you apprehend."

"Cool motive, but still a crime," Mark said. "We arrested him for negligent property damage, but Miss Chen posted his bail shortly after. It seems her opinion of him extends beyond his art indeed."

"Rudy isn't a murderer," Poppy repeated. "I promise you! Now am I free to go?"

We left the interview room, leaving Poppy to walk free from the station. I'd now talked with each member of Zaza's inner clique, and I didn't have any strong feelings about any of them being the murderer.

"Is Rudy still here?" I said to Mark.

"No, he took off pretty swiftly. Sorry you didn't get a chance to talk with him."

"I've heard enough anyway. Rudy would only muddy the waters further."

As things stood, he was the only suspect that I couldn't place. Was he innocent or guilty? Good or bad? His reputation preceded him, and I'd quite happily go the rest of my life without seeing him again, but he *had* demonstrated that he used his magic for good when he captured that charity box thief.

"So, have you solved it?" Mark said to me. "How did Rudy do it?"

"Why are you so set on this being Rudy?"

"Because he doesn't have an alibi after he 'left' the museum. Everyone else is clearly innocent."

I half-suspected they were all innocent, but that didn't mean they weren't hiding something. The only clue we had so far was a broken window, and I distinctly remembered Rudy's torn jacket and bloody elbow.

Maybe he really was behind this.

8

"*Y*ou can't make me take that!" Artemis howled, turning to zip away before I spritzed him with Dr. Skull's Witchups remedy. "Get away from me!"

The little cat was normally fast and probably would have got away under normal circumstances. However, he was under the weather, and the Witchups seem to affect his reaction speed.

Artemis made a half-hearted attempt of getting away but wasn't fast enough for my lightning fast maneuvers. I whipped the spritz bottle out like it was pistols at dawn and managed to catch him in a cloud of the shimmering purple smoke. The charmed bottlecap spouted off another one of its pre-recorded advertisements.

"Having trouble performing magic in front of others? Try Dr. Skull's patented calm balm! The only balm proven to take off the edge!"

"Dr. Skull sure loves his balms," I said and handed the bottle over to Selena, while relaying the complicated times of administration to her.

"Ah, seems straight forward enough," she said. "I've used Dr. Skull's products in the past, they really are the best."

"I don't know what all the fuss is about," Artemis protested. "I'm really feeling much better. I don't need any more medicine, thank you very much." Not only did Artemis sound much more congested than this morning, but a great big sneeze followed his declaration of health.

Dozens of small golden fruit bowls covered the lounge floor. Each one was filled with a strange red liquid.

"Is that blood?" Selena asked.

"Cranberry juice," Artemis sniffed. "Don't ask me why."

"You're obviously not better," I said to him. "Let Selena look after you for the next few days and it won't be long until you're back to your old annoying self. Oh also, no more ice cream."

"What?"

"Rebecca from the drugstore told me you had an allergy. You should have told me. You've brought this on yourself."

"I'd rather die!" Artemis cried. I rolled my eyes and petted him on the head.

"Just make sure you rest up and be nice to Selena."

"Selena?!" Artemis said. "You mean you're not sticking around to look after me?"

"She's doing more than a good job I think." Also I couldn't see any teabags stapled to the walls, bolstering my confidence that Selena was slowly on the mend.

"Don't worry Chelsea, I've got this. Artemis has my undivided attention. I will have to nip upstairs in a bit to peel back all the wallpaper and freshen up the paste but I—" She stopped herself. "Wait, that's crazy talk again isn't it?"

"Just a little!" I laughed nervously.

"How are things with Adam by the way?" she asked. "Do you have any plans moving forward for that?"

"Harper gave me that ring that lets me access the shifter ranch at any time. I thought I might go and check out the village in the day, it might seem a little less intimidating. Do you know Adam well?"

"I'd say we're good acquaintances. There's not a ton of room on this island so shifters end up running into one another eventually."

"Then you know him well enough to see he's not acting like himself?"

"Oh for sure. He's acting totally bonkers. Melody, that pretty white-haired girl he claims to be in love with, she is too as a matter of fact. I've known her for a while, and she's usually not this…"

"Stupid?"

"That's the word. They're both acting plain stupid. I can't figure out what's got into them."

"Do you know the rest of the pack well? Any idea if someone has a vendetta against either of them?"

"I know this upcoming ceremony is supposed to be important. I'm not sure what it involves exactly, but they *really* need the chalice for it."

"And when is that?"

"The next full moon. End of next week I think."

Yikes. That didn't give us much time at all. If I wanted more information it looked like my only options were to go back to the shifter ranch and do some looking around, the only problem was that I still didn't have a car, and my usual ports of call—Lizzy and Deacon— were both ruled out.

A call came in on my cell. I saw it was my Aunt Glenda, hesitated for a moment and then answered. "Hello?"

"Do you have any experience with bare-knuckle boxing?"

"…No. Why?"

I heard a disappointed huff down the line. "No reason. I just finished watching Fight Club and thought it looked like fun."

"You want to start an illegal underground bare-knuckle fight club?"

Glenda laughed down the line. "Who, me? No!" More laughter followed and then she composed herself. "The judge said if I did that again it would be prison for sure. But there's nothing to stop you… ah, forget about it."

How was I related to this woman?

"The wool shop is quiet today then?" I asked. Glenda, my eccentric aunt, was a little haywire. She ran *Wicked Wools* in the center of town and looked like a sweet and dumpy middle-aged woman, but you only had to talk with her for a few seconds to realize she was stark raving crazy.

"It's always quiet when it's raining." I glanced out the window and saw it was in fact raining again. "That's when I usually put Fight Club on and admire Mr. Pitt's fine abdominal resume."

"Why not give me a hand?" I said. "I'm not interested in a fight club, but there are a pack of werewolves that want my gardener dead, so I'm trying to figure that one out."

"You need a ride?" she asked, her voice suddenly much more interested.

"Always. Do you have much experience with werewolves? Can you help?"

More laughter. "Oh honey, I'll have those puppies eating out of my hand in no time. It's not the hidden place over in the woods is it?"

"Yeah, the alpha, Harper, gave me a ring so I can get in whenever I like."

"I'll be there in five minutes."

"It's a fifteen minute drive from your shop!"

"Five minutes!"

The line went dead.

I really needed to sort out a car.

"I'm just saying, I think the aim of driving is to not go at full speed perhaps *all* of the time!"

I held on for dear life as Glenda threw her car around another blind corner, her little car sliding around like we were in a movie about illegal street racing.

"Speed's fun darling!" Glenda laughed, whooping and hollering to herself as she weaved through three cars. "Anyway, when's your momma getting here?"

"How did you know she was coming?" I asked. So far, my mother had only announced her intention to visit with me on the phone, and I didn't think she was on speaking terms with Glenda.

"Oh, any able-bodied Sponks woman develops a keen ability to detect your mother from afar. It's best to always stay alert of course. I have finely tuned my body over the years, the hairs on the back of my neck begin to stand whenever she gets within a hundred miles of the island."

"You guys really don't get on, huh?" I asked. Mom had never really spoken about her sister's much, and I didn't think she really had a relationship with any of them.

"Don't get me wrong," Glenda said, "I love my little sister Lorelai, I just think the world would be much safer with her back in the fires of hell. No offense darling, I think you're lovely of course."

"None taken." Truthfully speaking my mom was a handful. I understood why Glenda would be wary of her visiting. I felt the same way. "She's not given any clues yet, other than a picture taken at LAX a few days ago. Mom isn't the type to give any helpful clues, like a date or a time, or a place."

"I can feel it in my bones. My blood is starting to crawl south. She's near all right." I glanced over at Glenda and saw a wild and distant look in her eye, like some warrior gearing up for battle with a great beast. "I'll be ready Lorelai." She whispered to herself. "This time… you'll see."

"Anyway," I said, wanting to steer the conversation towards something a little less ominous.

"Yes! Anyway!" Glenda snapped out of her trance. "How's this business with Deacon? I heard Magical Crimes Investigation are keeping an eye on him. He found out you're a witch."

My mouth opened, no words coming out as I found myself stupefied. "How do you possibly know everything that is going on in my life right now?"

Glenda chuckled. "Well I'm always keeping an eye on the horizon to watch out for your momma, and I bugged the MCI years ago. I intercept all of their communications and keep a very close eye on their activity."

"You're spying on the magical police?!"

"Of course, I don't trust a single one of those idiots. Now I've managed to relax a little since you moved to the rock, seems like you've got them whipped into place, but they couldn't find water if they fell out of a boat."

"Wait, so you've been spying on them. Chad has his little invisible pixie friends spying on Deacon. Do you know where he is? Do you know what's going on?" Glenda looked at me for a second, her lips pursed tight. She opened her mouth then closed it again. She did know something. "What? What is it?"

"Look darling, I shouldn't have brought it up. Why don't we just enjoy the rest of this peaceful drive? We're nearly at the ranch."

Glenda's car momentarily lifted off the ground as we went racing over the top of a hill. My knuckles turned white, gripping the hand-holds tightly until the wheels came back down a second later.

"Please just tell me what you know," I said. "This might be my last car ride ever!"

She rolled her eyes and sighed. "The women in this family, honestly! Drama queens! The lot of you! But fine… Deacon has gone up to Delfino. Chad's little spy friends followed him up there."

"Delfino." So the Stark brothers had it right. Or partly right at least. "For police training?"

"I'm not sure exactly. I only get a fuzzy image on an old tube monitor back at my house. I charmed it to spy on MCI magic streams. There's been a few flickers of Chad's invisible friends as they follow Deacon. Last I saw he'd pulled his car up outside Bedlam."

"Bedlam?"

"Well Delfino is a sleepy little surfer town, I'm sure you know that, but it also has a psychiatric facility up in the hills. It's world-renowned you know! All the celebrities fly out here and check themselves in whenever they have a breakdown."

"Wait, Deacon thinks he's going crazy? He's checked himself into a mental hospital?"

Glenda suddenly brought her car into a sudden stop, yanking the wheel sharply to the right and skidding onto the gravel track outside of the empty paddock hiding the shifter ranch.

"Looks like it. Now shall we interrogate some puppies before they behead your gardener?"

"Witchy gods help me," I muttered to myself.

Dean was at the gate again, but this time he had no issue letting me inside. He did still slightly as he saw Glenda with me.

"Glenda?!" he said. He looked at me. "Why did you bring her?!"

"She has a car, and I don't."

"Oh, okay." Dean looked very nervous indeed. "I need to go and speak to Harper!"

Dean ran off into the village as Glenda and I stepped through the gate. "What's his problem?" I asked. "It looked like he's terrified of you."

"Everyone on this rock acts like they're terrified of me darling, I have no idea why." I could think of a few reasons. "Where to first?"

"I planned on checking with Harper first, just to let him know we are here."

"The alpha himself. How exciting. Let's go!"

Glenda and I walked through the village, following the winding woodland paths to the hall at the very back of the settlement. A couple of wary glances came our way from the shifter men and women that were getting on quietly with their days, but no one came up to us or said anything.

If I didn't know any better, I'd think Glenda had a history with these people, but she did have something of a reputation on the island, and it was possible they were just scared of her on assumption.

I led Glenda inside the large cabin and followed the hallways to the workshop where we met Harper last time. He was there once again, dealing with a panicked looking Dean. Both of the men jumped as we entered.

"Oh! So, it's true!" Harper said, glancing over uneasily at Glenda. He shot an irritated look at Dean. "I told my packmate Dean here that he must be mistaken, an esteemed guest like the great warrior Glenda Sponks surely wouldn't have come here to see this village."

"Just giving my niece a ride," Glenda commented, looking around the workshop. "What are you making there? A cabinet? Those dovetail joints are nicely done."

Harper laughed nervously. It was a little amusing to see the giant alpha so out of his element. "Forgive my manners," he said. "Would you like food or drink? We have venison, berries, and our own craft beer."

"That all sounds good," Glenda said, walking across the shop to pick up a handsaw. "Pile it up homeboy. Now these joints look good, but they could be neater."

"I'll just look around by myself, Glenda?" I said.

"Huh? Oh yes, honey. Just come and shout me when you're done. I have to teach this pup a thing or two about woodworking."

"Pup?!" Harper laughed. I got the impression if anyone else made that joke the shifter male would tear his clothes off and rip a chunk out of their throat. Was the giant alpha wolf smitten with my Aunt Glenda?

"Right, well… I'll just be far away from here," I said, keen to be far away from this bizarre bout of flirting. I re-traced the path back down to the cells from the other day and heard Melody and Adam before I saw them. I wasn't surprised to see the white-haired girl sitting on a stool on the open side of the bars.

"No, I think it's a brilliant idea!" she said, all giddy and excitable. "Just wait until Harper hears about this!"

"About what?" I asked, stopping by the cell to stare at the pair of smitten idiots.

"Oh Chelsea, you're back!" Adam enthused. "I just asked Melody to marry me, and she said yes! We're going to tell Harper straight away."

I wasn't quite sure, but I couldn't imagine Harper reacting positively to the 'good news.'

"Congratulations, but maybe keep it to yourselves for now. Harper does have a lot on his plate at the moment of course, what with this missing chalice and all."

Adam's face suddenly became much graver. "That's a great point Chelsea." He looked at Melody and sighed, the pair of them were holding hands through the bars. "Mellybean, maybe Chelsea is right. We don't want our good news overshadowed by the bad."

"Mellybean?"

"That's his nickname for me," Melody beamed. "I'm his Mellybean, and he's my Adam Bear."

"Excuse me, I just need to go upstairs and vomit for ten minutes. Listen guys, can we talk seriously for a moment, you're both not acting like yourselves. Can you think of anything that might have happened to turn you this way?"

"Love!" Melody said.

Adam nodded vigorously. "Love. It's love Chelsea, and we're not going to hide it!"

"Ugh…" I sighed.

"You're not going to get anywhere with the two of them," a voice said from the stairs. I turned and saw another girl with long white-hair standing at the opposite end of the corridor. "Melody, stop fooling around here and go and help in the field."

"But Nadine!—"

"Go," Nadine ordered, like a parent dealing with a moody teenager.

Melody and Adam shared their soppy goodbyes and Melody skulked out of the cells. Once she was gone Nadine came over to me. "Let's talk upstairs. The less these two hear the better."

"Who are you?" I asked as I followed her out of the cells.

"I'm Melody's older sister, Nadine. I heard Harper brought you in to try and figure out what's going on here. The pair of them are acting like morons, I take it you noticed?"

"Kind of hard to miss, any idea what's going on?"

"I think someone is messing with the pair of them. Trying to stir trouble. I know Adam a little, he definitely took that chalice, but the normal Adam wouldn't do that. And Melody? She's a smart girl, she's not some lovestruck teenager."

"Why would someone mess with them?" I asked.

"Kismet," Nadine answered plainly.

"Kismet?"

"Fate, destiny. It is the ceremony we hold at the end of next week, the Crowning of Kismet. We will assign the next female to lead our pack into the next generation, someone to serve alongside the ruling alpha."

"A new mate for Harper?" I asked.

Nadine shook her head. "No, Harper is stepping down. He is the one that called the ceremony. Once we have elected our new queen she will mate with Harper's successor, Gerard."

"How many female shifters are in the running for this new position?"

"Anyone who wants to put their name forward. There is Goldie, Rachel, Sabine, and Melody."

"Melody is in the running? She already seems pretty smitten with Adam."

"She has no choice, as part of the line we have to nominate one of our own. I already have a mate so I cannot participate. Melody has to take part."

"I see."

"And she is the current favorite. The rest of our pack want our family to carry on with a leading capacity, but Melody doesn't want to. She is not destined for Gerard."

"Why is Harper stepping down?" I asked.

"His mate, Shasha, she died of an illness several years ago. Since then his desire to lead has diminished, hence him calling for a new ceremony."

"But then Adam turns up and steals the chalice, which I'm guessing is an important element."

"Crucial."

"So… Melody is going to be the next queen of this pack, whether she likes it or not. Adam took the chalice to stop that from happening, and now they're both acting weird."

"Someone is doing this deliberately," Nadine said. She stopped and looked around. "I found this. I think it's a clue. You're a witch. Can you help? Do you know what it is?"

She handed me a small red orb filled with shimmering liquid. It had an unusual aroma. "No idea, but I can try and find out," I said as I pocketed it. "Any more clues?"

"No, but I hope you figure this out soon. My sister needs your help, just as much as your friend."

"Someone obviously doesn't want Melody to take the queenhood." But who? The new alpha? One of the other women opting for the position?

Just then another call came through on my cell, this time from an unknown number. I answered the call and heard heavy breathing.

"Chelsea Sponks?" the voice said, low and distorted.

"Yes. Who is this?"

"A concerned friend of Rudy Malkin's. He's innocent, and I can prove it. I can give you an alibi. He was with me that night."

"Go on," I said.

"The old mint ball warehouse by the docks, tonight at eight. Come alone."

The line went dead.

9

"Oh heck, nah," Lizzy said as we pulled up outside the old abandoned mint ball warehouse. The sun had set, and it was nighttime again on Pendle Island. We arrived at the old docks just as the anonymous person on the phone requested, and it was definitely spooky.

Pendle Island was infamous for occasional bouts of mist and tonight unhelpfully proved no exception. A wall of creepy mist rolled across the abandoned warehouses, illuminating brightly in the white shafts of light coming from Lizzy's head lights.

"This has bad idea written all over it!" she said. "Let's just go back to town and get dinner, like you promised!"

"We'll get dinner back at my house. Let's see this through first. Someone obviously has information that can help the case, and they didn't want to go to the police, so there must be a good reason." I climbed out of the car and Lizzy regretfully followed me.

"Shouldn't we have long trench coats and trilby hats for a meeting like this?" Lizzy asked. "It would at least complete the picture."

"Feel free to magic one up if you want," I said. We entered through the open doors of the old abandoned warehouse, and everything suddenly seemed to go still. I whispered a spell to myself, one that I had been working on recently. *"Noctis!"*

"Good idea," Lizzy whispered, repeating the spell herself.

A small blip echoed through my head and the change came about. The magical pulse of warmth shimmered over my eyes and the room suddenly got brighter. Noctis was a spell to help with night vision. I couldn't see in the dark completely, but the darkest shadows were certainly a bit brighter, and I could now make out the shape of the room and its contents.

There was lots of old machinery and rusted metal tanks, stretching high up into the vaulted ceilings. The room itself was large, the old roof marred with holes that dripped water from the outside elements.

"There!" Lizzy said, pointing at a figure that slunk forward from the darkness.

"You're the one that phoned?" I said to the figure. They didn't say anything at first. They just stumbled forward in the shadows, one hand clutched tightly against their torso.

Did they have a gun?

"Hey, talk!" Lizzy shouted. "Or we will defend ourselves!"

The shadow stumbled forward another couple of steps, their free hand holding onto a piece of machinery to steady themselves. They stepped into a beam of moonlight that poured down from the decrepit ceiling.

It was Verity Newport.

"Run!" she said, gasping the word before she tumbled forward and hit the ground. Lizzy and I both ran towards her at once and saw her coat was soaked through was blood. Her eyes were glassy and unblinking, staring up at stars through the holes in the warehouse ceiling.

Lizzy checked for a pulse, shook her head and looked at me. "She's dead Chelsea."

I closed my eyes and sighed. "Call the police."

We had another murder on our hands.

The police arrived not long after that, and Lizzy and I waited in her car, listening to the Hamilton soundtrack on repeat while we watched rain run down the windshield. In the distance were the torches of the police searching the warehouse.

Eventually a knock came at my window and I nearly jumped through the roof. I saw Mark—or Clark, I could never tell them apart—standing on the opposite side with a cheery smile. I wound the window down and turned off the music.

"Any clues, Mark?" I guessed.

"Clark actually. She's definitely dead."

Lizzy and I looked at one another. "We'd figured that much. Anything else? A murder weapon? Footprints?"

Clark chuckled. "Oh, that stuff! Yeah. None of that. Looks like a ghost in the night job. One of the forensics say it's a stab wound from the looks of it. Can you run me over the events once again?"

"I received an anonymous phone call from someone saying that Rudy was innocent, and they could provide an alibi for him. I came here with Lizzy and then Verity Newport literally stumbled out of the shadows and dropped dead."

"She say anything?"

"I don't think so."

"She told us to run," Lizzy reminded me.

"She did!" I said, suddenly remembering. This wasn't my first time dealing with a dead body, but it was the first time I'd seen someone actively die in front of me, so I was a little shaken.

"Interesting," Clark said. "Well… we'll tape the scene off and tidy things up. I haven't got any more questions for you now. You two should head home and get out of this rain. Looks like it's going to come down hard tonight."

Clark and I nodded our goodbyes before I rolled up the window and Lizzy pulled her car away from the spooky warehouse. When we finally got back to my place the rain was indeed coming down hard. We hurried inside and saw Old Mad John sat in the hallway chair, reading a newspaper he had grabbed from off the side. He didn't even look up, but he did offer a lazy, "Get out?"

"Yeah, another great day of tripping over dead bodies John, thanks for asking," I said. Lizzy and I both made our way into the kitchen and I was relieved to see everything in its normal place. Selena was sat at the table reading a copy of *Witch's Digest.*

"Guys!" she said. "How was the day?"

"Oh, the same old lunacy. How is Artemis? Has he been taking his medicine?"

"Every dose," she smiled. "I had to pin him down the first few times, but he's resigned himself to it now. I think he's already getting better; he's certainly sneezing less."

"That's a relief. What about you?"

"I resisted a strong urge to plug all the faucets with tile grout. I think having something to focus on is helping my shifter sickness. In fact, I think I'm almost back to normal!"

"That's great! Listen, Lizzy and I are going to order take out. You want to get in on this?"

"Could do. I did make soup. It's in the stockpot on the hob if you want any."

"Soup?" I cast a wary look at Lizzy and went over to the stockpot. As I pulled back the lid, I saw a pair of wellington boots half-melted in gravy. I turned around and looked back at Selena. "Not quite sure you're all the way healed Selena. Why don't we just order Chinese?"

"Suits me fine! I can get some Tupperware and box up the soup for tomorrow."

"That… that sounds like a great plan," I said with a sigh of defeat.

One hour later I wolfed down the last mouthful of my Chinese food and finished melting into the couch. I muttered a cleaning spell I had been practicing and watched in delight as the empty trays and dirty dishes carried themselves into the kitchen.

Selena kicked up from the armchair by the fire and yawned a goodnight. "I better hit the hay; I was going to rotate all the trees in the backyard tomorrow. I've got a long day ahead of me!"

Once she was gone Lizzy questioned it. "Okay. Rotate the trees? What does that even mean?"

"She mentioned something about it earlier," Artemis said, clawing his way out of a bag of wool underneath one of the footstools. I hadn't even realized he was in there. "She wants to dig up the trees, rotate them and plant them again so they 'get enough sun.'"

"Definitely still sick," I muttered to myself. "And how are you, Artemis?"

Artemis sneezed and a fountain of golf balls started to bounce down from a hole in the ceiling. Lizzy quickly patched the magical leak with a counter spell.

"Never better," he asked. "Have you freed the oaf yet? Or have the wolves torn him to pieces?"

"No luck yet, though we do have one clue." I caught Lizzy and Artemis up to speed with the trouble at the shifter ranch so far, producing the tiny red orb as I reached the end of the story. "Any ideas?" I asked as I held it up for them to see.

Lizzy shook her head. "No, looks like a bath bomb though."

"It's an orb of inhibition," Artemis yawned.

"An orb of inhibition?" we both asked in turn.

He nodded. "Yeah. It's kind of like a smoke bomb. You throw it down and anyone caught in the fumes comes out the other side acting like they're drunk."

"Permanently?" I asked.

"Eh… It lasts about a week or so," he said. "They're not super difficult to make. Just some poppy flowers and a little bit of spite. You have to be careful around them though, if you're not you can end up getting caught in the smoke too."

Suddenly I found myself not wanting to be near this little orb. I held it at arm's length, feeling as though it was a live grenade. "Can someone put this somewhere safe?!"

"Cincinno," Lizzy said, and she snapped her fingers. A lattice of golden light appeared in the air around the orb and it disappeared with a 'pop!' sound.

"So, someone in the shifter camp has deliberately spiked Adam and

Melody to make them act stupider, and it's got something to do with this upcoming ceremony. Now I just need to talk to a few more people and figure out why someone would do such a thing."

"You'll need an orb of clarity too," Artemis pointed out. "To help restore affected individuals back to normal."

"Is that hard to make?" I asked.

"No, but you'll need some Lapis Rose. That's the magical opposite of a poppy."

I looked at Lizzy. "Do you know where I can get that?"

"Don't look at me, that's not an easy plant to find!"

A slow and evil-sounding chuckle came from Artemis. We both looked at him.

"Something funny, Artemis?" I asked.

"Oh, how the tables have turned. It just so happens I have some in my personal store."

"Cool, so you can make the orbs then."

"That depends. When am I likely to see chocolate fudge ice cream again?" he said.

"Are you really trying to barter with me right now? You sneezed earlier and nearly got knocked out by a falling watering can."

"The key word there is *nearly*, Chelsea."

"The point is that you're not having any more ice cream, but maybe we can reach a mutual agreement. What about sorbet? That's cold and full of sugar."

"Sorbet?" he said, one of his little cat brows raised in question. "This sorbet, is it like ice cream?"

"No," Lizzy answered.

"Yes," I said quickly after. I shot her a look and she corrected herself.

"Oh, yes! Definitely yes. It's just like ice cream. Sorbet. Hm. Yummy."

"Very convincing," I said to my cousin.

"Glad to be of help."

"I'll try it," Artemis said. "But if it's no good we'll be having words. You can't keep ice cream away from me forever."

"I can and will." I looked at Lizzy again. "Are you staying over again tonight?"

"No, I need to go. I'm supposed to be looking after Bash's dog, Buster, and I said I'd pick him up before I went home."

"Dog?" Artemis said. "Yuck. Make sure you shower before you see me again."

"Maybe I'll just feed you to him?" she teased as she jumped out of her chair. "Do you need a lift anywhere tomorrow, Chelsea?"

"Actually, I was wondering if I could borrow your car. I need to take a short trip to Delfino."

"Ooh, sounds fun. Surfing?"

"Springing my boyfriend out of a mental hospital."

Lizzy's smile faltered. "…Okay. I'll bring the car around tomorrow. Drop me off at work before you go?"

After I said goodbye to Lizzy, I made my way upstairs and had a quick shower, which was otherwise uneventful apart from the fact that there was an old tire in the sink. I paid it no mind and tried to relax for five minutes. Once I was dry, I climbed into bed and read while listening to the rain against my bedroom window.

There was something so relaxing about hearing a storm outside.

I should have known better than to check my phone when it buzzed on my bedside table. Sure enough I saw another cryptic message from my mother:

Back together soon! Can't wait to see my daughter!

I decided to chance it and send a message back:

When are you coming?

Mom wasn't usually the type to reply within any helpful time-frame, but to my surprise she did, straight away:

Ending it with Marko tomorrow! He doesn't like coconut. What?!

The message was punctuated by a string of laughing emojis. I was somewhat impressed my mother had figured out emojis, and not at all surprised to learn nothing new about her visit. I would have better luck getting blood from a stone.

I let out my last sigh of the day and rolled over, only to be treated to a devastatingly loud blast of saxophone as soon as my head hit the pillow. I screamed in surprise and fell backwards out of bed, landing on the floor in a tangle as I looked up at my headboard in confusion.

There I saw one of the little tiny red jazz lizards that had escaped from Chad's coat a few days earlier. I cursed the lanky wizard, muttered a spell under my breath and a small glass bottle suddenly encased the noisy little lizard.

I grabbed a hairpin and poked some holes in the cork stoppering the top, turning the bottle over in my hands as I inspected the fiery little lizard. The muted sounds of furious jazz blasted from inside as the lizard scuttled around, looking for a way out.

"Why don't you chill out in there for the night, Coltrane," I said. "I'll give you to Artemis in the morning, he'll know what to do with you."

I finally lay my head on the pillow and turned off the light. My thoughts naturally returned to the main case at hand. Two people were dead now. Someone had killed Verity Newport. They wanted to erase Rudy's alibi.

But why?

1 0

elfino was one of the three main towns on Pendle Island. There was Pendle town in the south, the 'capital' which was frequently blasted by showers of torrential rain. Further up on the west coast was Delfino, a little sunny surfer town that seemed to get all the sunshine.

Further up after that was Babonix, a snowy town in the mountains.

The island was unusual that it had these little microclimates, but it was pretty handy if you ever wanted a reliable change of weather. At most the three towns were half an hour away from one another, and it wasn't too tricky to drive over. I'd spent a little bit of time in Babonix about a month ago when I was trapped in a ski lodge, but I'd only been in sunny Delfino briefly, and that ended with me finding a body on the beach.

The morning somehow went smoothly enough, which was a miracle at the moment with Artemis and Selena both messing up my house on an hourly basis. I left the little jazz lizard with Artemis before I ran outside to meet Lizzy, and then I drove the pair of us across town for a sugar breakfast and some existential dread with Sophia at her bakery.

After breakfast I dropped Lizzy off at the music studio and started the half hour drive up to Delfino. The drive was coastal for the most part and not short of breath-taking scenery. I made the mistake of checking out the local talk radio for the first time. The island wasn't large, so the pickings were slim. After a few channels of static, I found something: *Conspiracy hour with Ted and Todd.*

"That's just the thing Ted!" Todd said. "The government plan to put a microchip in every pen and pencil, that way—"

"They can always see what you're writing!"

"Exactly dude! And once they have that information well, there goes another one of our rights! Now that ties in nicely to our next segment, listener mail! Our first letter this week is from 'DingDong-Danny' and they say that Chocolate Yeti breakfast cereal is actually an alien mind-control device, designed to—"

"Maybe I'll drive in silence and enjoy the scenery," I said to myself as I clicked the radio off.

Before long I arrived in the sunny little town of Delfino. I did wonder how I was going to find the mental hospital, but I spotted the large building perched on the hilltop over the town. I drove through Delfino town center, the sidewalks packed full of happy surfers and folks with golden bronze skin.

"I really need to come out here for a week and work on my tan," I muttered to myself.

I followed the road through and out the other side of town. It quickly started to wind uphill through tall pine forests, and I knew the only thing at the end of this road was the mental hospital. I quietly thought to myself that the correct term these days was most likely psychiatric facility. As long as I didn't use the words 'loony bin' I was probably in the clear.

After another few minutes of driving I came around a final corner of trees and the sure enough the hospital came into view. I pulled up in the parking lot and was just about to get out when I saw —Deacon!

Deacon walked out of the front door of the hospital, a man in a long white jacket accompanying him. They talked for a moment and shook hands before Deacon carried on towards the lot. It was now or never, so I jumped out of the car and shouted at him.

"Deacon!" I said. "Over here!"

He looked over at me straight away and seemed very confused. I half expected him to run away again, but thankfully he came over. I ran around the car to meet him, but we stopped a couple of feet short of one another.

"Chelsea? How on earth did you—" He paused, perhaps sensing that magic had helped me find him. "What are you doing here?"

"I came here to talk to you," I said. "I wanted to ask you the same thing. Deacon you are not crazy, I promise you."

"I know that… well. I do now. Got a clear stamp of mental health. I'm sane. Or… as sane as everyone else makes out to be. Which means that you were…"

"I was telling the truth, and everything you saw in my kitchen was real." I looked around the lot and lowered my voice, even though we were the only ones out here. "Magic… magic is real."

"I'm starting to realize that is true too," he said. "Look, I was actually heading back to Pendle town today. I was coming back to see you. I'm sorry I ran out on you like that, and I'm sorry I've been avoiding your calls."

"I just wanted to know you're okay. Look, I know I've been hiding this big secret from you, and I'm sorry, but it's all quite new to me too, and I'm not even supposed to let regular folk know!"

He chuckled. "Looks like you're doing a standup job. If I'm being honest this isn't all a huge surprise to me. I was born on this island, and some of the things I've seen… well. Magic would *have* to be real to explain a lot about Pendle Island. It's not just you, is it, there are others on the island?"

"I mean I don't have a census or anything, but yes, there are quite a few more witches and wizards living here."

He nodded and let out a deep breath. "I wanted to sit down somewhere and get a drink to talk about this, but let's just get it out in the open here. I didn't run away because I'm afraid of you or this new information. I ran away because I'm afraid of myself."

"You… what?"

"I've never told anyone this before, and I'm almost certain no one else knows. When I was younger my dad tried to kill my mom because he thought she was an evil witch. Well, she wasn't. Turned out he had developed an undiagnosed mental illness and was suffering from hallucinations. He lives here now, in the hospital." He nodded to the building behind him.

"You thought you were going crazy too," I said.

"Sure did," he said with a nervous chuckle. "I thought this was a good opportunity to come and get my head checked. The doctors have always said my father's condition isn't hereditary, but I guess I always feared the same would happen to me. When I found out about your secret well… I guess I worried I was going down the same path. I don't want to hurt you Chelsea. I don't want to hurt anyone."

I didn't know what to say, I just jumped forward and threw my arms around him. "I'm sorry," I said. "This must be so confusing."

He laughed and hugged me back. It felt good to have him back again. "Just a little, but Chelsea, I want you to know, this doesn't change how I feel about you at all. In fact, it only makes you more intriguing. I have questions, so many questions—"

"You and me both," I said as I pulled back. "Look, I'm not kidding when I said I'm new to this. I only found out about magic when I moved to the rock. The one thing I do know is that you can't tell anyone about this. How much do the doctors know?"

"Nothing," he said. "Chelsea, I'm a cop. I've come across enough secrets over the years that I know when I'm supposed to keep something to myself. I gave them just enough information to voice my concerns, but nothing specific. I ran away pretty fast, but I heard you ask me not to tell anyone."

I breathed a sigh of relief. "I think we're good then." That was a big weight off my shoulders. "Deacon, you will not believe the week I'm having."

"More trouble in paradise? Surely not. What's the ticket this time?"

"Two dead bodies and a—" I paused, instinctively stopping myself before I said anything about Adam. "Actually… I guess I don't have to keep secrets from you now. Two dead bodies and trouble with my gardener. A local werewolf pack is holding him prisoner."

Deacon blinked a couple of times before letting out another nervous laugh. "Werewolves are real?"

"Oh, my darling Deacon. Welcome to my world of crazy. Shall we go home?"

He took my hand and kissed me. "Let's."

11

We drove back in our separate cars, arriving at the police station shortly after. Once inside we went into Deacon's office and I caught him up on the case. We may also have made out a little bit. I don't kiss and tell.

"Quite the doozy," he said as he closed the manilla folder holding the case details. "How have the Stark brothers been handling it?"

"Oh, you have some real professionals on your hands."

He laughed. "That bad, huh? Well what's your take on it?"

"All signs point to Rudy. The Stark brothers said the only piece of evidence at the crime scene was a broken window and glass. I saw Malkin later that night and he had a bloody elbow. Claimed he came off his bike. The emerald sculpture Zaza was going to present was missing."

"Robbery gone wrong?" Deacon suggested.

"The most likely theory, but the question is who."

"I'll admit Malkin is definitely my first hunch. The guy has been nothing but trouble for this island. Now this Verity Newport is dead too, it's not looking good."

"But she called to give me an alibi about Rudy. She said she was with him after he left the museum. But why do that in secret?"

"I suppose she didn't want the relationship to be public. Maybe she and Malkin are in this together somehow, she got spooked and tried to cook up an alibi. He got to her before she could blow their cover."

"Look I know he's trouble," I said after a long moment of reflection, "but is he a killer?"

"What do you mean?" Deacon asked, his brow furrowed in confusion. I glanced back at his office door to make sure it was closed and then I told him.

"Rudy is like me, he's a wizard."

"That guy?!" Deacon said in surprise.

"I know, I know. But it's true. Here's the other thing, he's kind of a dark wizard."

"Well that settles it then! He's evil, he must be guilty!"

"No, he uses magic to cause disruption, but only against those that deserve it." I explained how he helped catch the charity box thief.

"I see," Deacon said. "So, he's like a vigilante type."

"I guess that's a good word for it yeah."

He made an unhappy sound. "Vigilantes aren't good. People should never take the law into their own hands. Too many things can go wrong. What if this is another case of Malkin trying to be the law? Zaza LaFoo stiffed him and other artists on their work, Malkin confronts him, it goes wrong and he takes the sculpture as payment."

I took a breath to try and defend Rudy, but no words came to mind. Deacon was only painting logical conclusions. Rudy wasn't in a good position, and his attitude certainly didn't help things.

"Maybe we should go and talk with him, together," I said. "There's something missing here, and as soon as we figure it out, we're one step closer to solving all of this."

"Why don't we take the cruiser?" he said. "I can put the sirens on and everything."

My mouth dropped in excitement. "Really?!"

He chuckled and got up from his desk. "Come on, let's hit the road partner."

Ten minutes later we pulled up in a part of town nicknamed 'COHIP', which was an abbreviation of 'Coffee & Hipsters.' COHIP was five square blocks of coffee shops, hip bars and over-priced lofts. Lizzy's apartment wasn't actually too far from here. She was 'far enough away from the hipsters, but close enough to party with them.'

Deacon pulled up outside a small coffee shop named 'Alibaba Roast' and we climbed out of the car. Everywhere I looked I saw young art types, men with long beards, women with long hippy dresses—some of which I liked—some tie-dye and a few dream catchers dangling in shop windows.

"Malkin has a loft down here," Deacon said as he led us down a side alley next to the shop. "He's one of these types that lives amongst his work."

"I figured this area would be too gentrified for him, he seems like the type that would have a cabin out in the middle of nowhere."

"COHIP wasn't always like this," Deacon said. "Ten years ago, it was blocks and blocks of empty warehousing. A lot of money has come to the island in recent years and we've been fortunate enough to see development. Malkin's been here a while, finds himself straight in the center of hipster central now. I bet he hates it." He chuckled to himself.

We ducked inside a patchwork metal door and found ourselves in a small atrium, a locked elevator in front of us and a comm panel on the wall. Deacon pushed a button; the panel rang and Malkin answered.

"I told you Devira we're through, no amount of marble cake is going to make up for that."

"Malkin this is Sheriff Long. I'm here with Chelsea Sponks. Care to let us in so we can talk?"

Rudy sighed down the comm. "Make it quick," he said. "I'm in the zone."

The elevator in front of us clicked and Deacon pulled back the black metal grating. We stepped onto the large platform and it went up several floors. It immediately brought us into a wide and open loft full of the most amazing artwork. Rudy was at the very back of the loft, crouched at the bottom corner of a giant portrait of a woman's face, applying finishing touches with a small brush.

He stood up and turned around to face us. He didn't have a shirt on. His hair was greasy and all over the place. He looked thin and hungry. There were bags under his eyes.

"This better be good," he said. "I've been trying to finish this piece for years and I finally found the inspiration." He looked at me. "You solve the case yet?"

"Trying my darndest," I answered, stepping close to admire the giant portrait. "This is pretty amazing. Who is it?"

Rudy shrugged. "Just some girl I used to know. What do you guys want?"

"I take it you heard about Verity Newport," I said. Rudy nodded.

"Tweedledee and Tweedledum already came to see me this morning. I told them I didn't know anything."

"Verity called me because she said you were innocent. She said she had an alibi for you, that you were with her after you left the museum."

Rudy pulled an unsure face. "With Verity?"

"You're saying that's a lie?" Deacon asked. "Girl gives you an alibi and you turn your nose up at it?"

Rudy considered it a moment and then changed his tune. "Actually yeah. I was with her. We were... romantically involved, or whatever."

"Why do I get the feeling you're lying about a false alibi?" Deacon said to him.

"Look Rudy, it appears that Verity was trying to help you out, but someone killed her before I could talk to her. That means someone is trying to send you down, they want you to take the fall for Zaza's death."

"I already said I didn't do it, and now I have an alibi. So, what's the problem?"

"What about the night Verity died? Where were you?" Deacon asked.

"I was at an open night mic in a café down the block. Your detective twins already asked me that this morning, and they verified as much."

So, Rudy didn't kill Verity. We knew that much at least. "Was Zaza in any kind of magical trouble?" I asked.

Rudy suddenly stilled and looked at Deacon. "Chelsea."

"Relax, he knows about it all now."

"Is that so?" Rudy laughed. "Well, Zaza and the rest of his crew had nothing to do with magic, they're all regular folk. The only people he pissed off are the people he ripped off, and of those there are plenty. Now if you'll excuse me, I think we've covered all the bases here, unless you guys want to waste more of my time?"

"We'll be in touch Malkin," Deacon said dismissively. "Don't go anywhere."

"Like I have anywhere better to be."

"One last thing," I said. "What was in the bag that night you went to visit Harper?"

Rudy rolled his eyes and sighed again. "Man, I'm really not entitled to an ounce of privacy around you, am I?"

"Was it the money you got from Poppy that night, do you have money troubles with the shifter clan?"

"Man, you are the worst detective ever," he said. "I was delivering something to him. Just something he needs for an upcoming ceremony. It has nothing to do with Zaza, I promise you."

"Okay, fine. Thanks for your time, Rudy."

"Yeah, yeah. Now buzz off, narc." Rudy snapped his fingers and a cigarette appeared in his hand. "My vibe has been seriously harshed."

Once we got back to the station Deacon and I said goodbye at the front of the building. "Why don't we get dinner together later?" he asked.

"Sounds good to me," I said, standing on my tiptoes to kiss him. "We can talk more about that other thing too, if you like. Whatever you want to know, I'll try and answer it."

"Maybe we'll do one question a day. I think I need time to slowly absorb all this new information. What are you doing with the rest of your day?"

"I need to pick Lizzy up at some point. I might go check up on my friend Adam against first. Artemis is supposed to be making this anti-dote thing, it's—ah it's hard to explain."

Deacon nodded and kissed me on the forehead. "Good luck and call me if you need me. See you later."

I skipped back down the station steps and drove Lizzy's SUV to the store to pick up some raspberry sorbet. I wasn't sure if Artemis would like this after all, but I knew if I came back to the house empty handed, he wouldn't hold up his end of the deal. When I got home and opened the front door Old Mad John skipped out bellowing 'Get out!' over and over like he was part of a Broadway chorus.

"A bit of variety, I like it!" I said as I headed through to the back to find Artemis. I expected to find my familiar in the lounge, which had become his ward of sorts, but instead I only found Selena, she was asleep on the couch with a shovel in her hands. She stirred as I turned to leave.

"Oh, Chelsea, you're back!"

"Yes. Where is Artemis? Has he been taking his medicine?"

"He's in the shed at the bottom of the garden. He said he needed space to work on this spell for you. Medicine? Oh, yes! He's had every dose so far today. I just lay down to rest my eyes and fell asleep for five minutes, sorry."

"No worries." If Selena was asleep, she couldn't mess up the house. "Let's see how Artemis is getting on. What's the shovel for?"

Selena looked surprised to see the shovel in her hands. "I have no idea," she laughed. "Heh. I'll just… go put this back."

I walked out back and across the field of dirt that was now my back garden. If anything, it would give Adam plenty to work on when he finally came back. At the very bottom of the garden there was a shed and workshop, which he had turned into a cabin. He'd been staying in the cabin at the bottom of the garden ever since he started working for Griselda, and I had yet to step inside.

A bright flash of purple light came through the windows and I approached the front door, which was slightly ajar. I heard Artemis sneezing and cursing to himself.

"Knock, knock," I said as I stepped inside. I pushed the door open and saw a cozy looking cabin, with wooden furniture and a large wooden fireplace. Artemis was sitting on his back paws, a pair of half-moon spectacles on his face while he peered over the top of a large bubbling cauldron.

"I need peace and quiet!" he demanded. "Oh, it's just you Chelsea. I thought it was Selena again. She's been driving me crazy."

"Someone talking *your* ear off?" I laughed as I stepped inside the cabin. "Now that must be a first."

"The girl is lovely, Chelsea, don't get me wrong, but she is also completely bonkers. She makes me look like a sane person!"

"And that's saying something," I stepped in closer and peered over the bubbling cauldron. "How are the orbs of clarity coming along?"

"What?" he said, looking at me in confusion. "Oh, those things? They're done. They're on the table behind you."

Looking back, I saw a small velvet bag on the table. I picked it up and looked inside to see two small balls of shimmering green. "So, I just throw these on the ground and Adam and Melody are cured?"

"Sure are," Artemis muttered. He was reading something from a giant magical textbook, not really paying much attention to me anymore.

"Say, what are you doing?" I asked.

"Oh, just tinkering. I don't break out the cauldron much these days, so it's always fun to experiment when I do. The recipes in these books are always so crumby, my own variations are far superior."

"What are you making now?" I asked.

"Potion of invisibility," he answered. "But get this, I'm swapping out the nirn root for black cap mushrooms."

"Is it safe to change magical recipes like that?"

"Perfectly!" he said. "Just watch! Cauldron, serve it up!"

Artemis tapped his paw against the side of the cauldron three times and three glass bottles suddenly hovered up from the bubbling liquid and settled themselves on the side. Artemis grabbed one in his mouth and tilted his head back, drinking the whole thing down. A loud 'pop!' snapped through the cabin and he vanished.

A second later he popped back.

He turned green.

Smoke started to pour out of his ears.

He flickered in and out like an old TV set.

Finally, Artemis hovered up into the air and grew ten times in size until he was the size of a large lion. He crashed back down onto the table and the entire cabin shook under his sheer weight.

"Artemis!" I shouted in alarm.

"Oh, this is not good," he said, his voice now sounding more like Barry White. He very slowly kept growing until there was almost no more room left to spare in the cabin. My cat was the size of a rhino.

"Artemis!" I shouted again, squished back against the front door because there was no more room.

"Unintended side effect," he said in his booming voice. "You have to admit though, this is kind of awesome."

"Is it?!"

The small cat popped his tongue against the roof of his mouth and vanished. Next thing I heard him outside. I hurried out of the cabin and found him prowling around on the giant dirt lawn. "Oh, this is great!" he roared. "Now I'm the king of Pendle Island! Look out other cats!"

"We'll figure this out later," I said. "I don't have time to deal with this right now. Just stay inside the house and make sure normal people don't see you."

"Hey, I could be the Pendle Puma now! I bet that pays well."

"I can't think of a single way it could," I said. "It's not like wild cats sign photographs at fan conventions."

"Ah, good point. I don't care about money though. Fame is the real drug."

"I *have* to go," I said, looking at my watch in a hurry. I barely had time to get back to the shifter ranch before I had to go and pick up Lizzy from work. "Just tell Selena what happened so she doesn't freak out when a giant cat walks in the door."

"Ha, good luck pinning me down for medication now!" he said, his giant voice booming through the forest. A giant sneezed followed his boasting and all of a sudden dozens of giant bowling shoes appeared in the air. One by one they fell down and sunk into my scalped lawn.

If I stayed any longer, I was going to pull all of my hair out.

"Bye!" I said cheerily, but inside I was close to having a meltdown. I ran around the side of the house and hopped back into Lizzy's car. I'd have to drive quick, but I could still get over to the shifter ranch and make it back to Lizzy in time.

Then my phone buzzed. It was a call from an unknown number.

I answered it.

"The old—*CLICK CLICK CLICK CLICK—tower.*"

"What?!" It sounded like someone was using a voice scrambler, and to top it off there was a high-pitched clicking on the call that kept echoing over the line.

"The—*CLICK CLICK CLICK CLICK—*clock."

"You'll have to call me back, there's a really strange interference on this line."

"Darn phone," the scrambled voice said. "Is that better?"

"Yes. Who is this?"

"You want answers about the—*CLICK CLICK—*case?"

"Answers about Zaza and Verity?"

"Yes—*CLICK CLICK.*"

"Yes, who is this?"

"Meet me at the old clock tower. Answers at the top—*CLICK CLICK CLICK—*You can close this case once and for all. Now."

The line went dead. I looked at my watch, sighed and put the car into gear, pulled down the drive and turned onto the road, heading in the direction of the old clock tower.

I don't know what I did in a past life to deserve all this intrigue in my life. Maybe I was a real pain in the butt?

I arrived at the old clock tower five minutes later. It was on the side of town near the old warehouses. Perhaps I should have been more cautious about this meeting, considering how my last one turned out, but I needed answers darn it, and I was going to get them!

I got out of the car and peeled back a loose section of chicken wire that fenced the clocktower off from the rest of the street.

"I'm here!" I announced to no one in particular, hoping this wasn't some complete waste of time. I stepped inside the old tower and found a staircase winding upwards. I followed it up to the top.

When I arrived at the top landing, I saw an envelope on the floor. I bent over to pick it up when someone stepped out of the shadows and pushed me. A scream left my mouth and I fell back, tumbling down the stairs as I tried to grab hold of anything.

My head hit something, and everything went dark.

12

I awoke to the gentle sound of clinical beeping. As I opened my eyes, I realized my head hurt like a mother. Everything was blurry and bright, and as my surroundings came into focus, I saw I was lying in a hospital bed on a busy ward.

"What the?" I muttered to myself.

"Chelsea!" Deacon said. "You're awake!"

"Yeah," I said slowly. I sat up in bed and noticed that everything hurt. "What happened?"

"We were hoping you could tell us," he said. "An anonymous caller sent an ambulance to the old clock tower and the paramedics found you unconscious at the bottom of the stairs."

Deacon handed me a glass of water and I took a sip, blinking a few times as I tried to shake the fog from my brain. I suddenly remembered the call and the push.

"Someone told me to meet them there," I recounted. "They said they could help close the case. When I got there, I saw an envelope on the floor at the top of the tower. I went to pick up the envelope when someone jumped out of the shadows and pushed me down the stairs."

"Did you see who it was?" Deacon asked anxiously.

I tried to recall, but I couldn't. "No. Just a blurry shape standing over me right before I passed out. How long have I been out?"

"The ambulance picked you up half an hour ago. The paramedics got your ID from your purse. They called Lizzy, who called me. She's in the waiting room. Only one visitor at the bedside out of hours. I should call for the doctor in fact." He stood up and pressed a button on the wall behind me. Thirty seconds later a young brunette woman with sharp blue eyes hurried onto the ward.

"Ah, Miss Sponks, you're awake! My name is Dr. Hill. You can call me Peggy." She immediately started looking over the various machines and readouts surrounding me. "How are you feeling? Can you remember what happened?" She took my pulse, checked my eyes and even looked in my ears as I answered.

I recalled what I had mentioned to Deacon and she listened intently.

"Sounds like quite a bad a fall but looking over your vitals it looks like you are pretty good at falling. I think we'd like to keep you in for observation over night, but I see no issue in letting you check out tomorrow. Can you identify your attacker?"

"No, I didn't even see their face."

"Well this would be classified as attempted murder, so I'd strongly encourage that you make a report to the po—" Peggy looked at Deacon and laughed. "I'm guessing you're already way ahead of this one."

"We'll find out who did this Chelsea, don't you worry," Deacon said. "No one's going to hurt you in here."

"I'm not worried. Let the coward try again! I'll take them this time!"

The doctor laughed nervously. "Visiting is open now," she said as she glanced down at her watch. "If you have anyone waiting outside, they can come in for an hour." Her sentence was barely finished when Lizzy came running through the doors with a giant teddy under her arms. She ran across the ward and swamped me in a giant hug, one that hurt a little.

"Easy, easy!" I winced.

"Sorry," Lizzy said as she pulled back. "I've been worried sick though. We all have."

"Just call if you need anything," the doctor said and left.

It appeared Lizzy wasn't the only one waiting. My Aunt Glenda approached the bed and Selena was here too.

"I knew you'd pull through cupcake," Glenda said. "We Sponks women are tough stuff."

"Where's Artemis?" I said to Selena.

"Oh, he's here," she answered. "I reversed the... *thing* he did, but I might have reversed it too much. He's... well..." Selena looked around and pulled something out of her pocket. Between her finger and thumb she held a little black cat that was no bigger than a cupcake.

"Chelsea!" he wailed in a high-pitched voice. "You have to help! She's shrunk me!"

Selena quickly stuffed the tiny cat back into her jacket pocket.

"Uh... is that fixable?" I said.

"I tried a few things in the waiting room," Glenda said, "but nothing is working so far."

"It's probably fixable," Lizzy said. "It's very rare for magic to be truly permanent. Oh, Deacon, how are you enjoying your intro to the world of magic?" Lizzy said.

I looked over to the ashy-faced Deacon, who seemed very confused by everything that was going on around him. He looked at me. "I picked up Lizzy when they called her. Obviously, her car was still at the old clock tower. She told me she was a witch too."

"I figured if he was back on the scene you guys must have patched things up," she said confidently. "And if not, he's getting blanked anyway!"

"Blanked?" Deacon said.

"You're not getting blanked," I said, rushing past the word. "Don't worry about that. The most dangerous thing on this island is every other woman in my family."

"Um, I am a delight," Glenda said. "That alpha is smitten with me, he wants me to be his warrior woman!"

"What alpha?" Lizzy said. "Are you snagging up all the hot singles again?!"

The visiting hour went quickly enough. It was sixty minutes of madness from start to finish, but that could be expected with Lizzy, Glenda and Selena making up the visiting party. Once everyone left Deacon stayed a little while longer and we shared some crumby hospital food while watching telenovelas on a screen that extended from the bed on a folding arm.

When nine came around Deacon had to leave, including the other guests on the ward. He arranged to come by tomorrow morning and pick me up when the doctors discharged me. There wasn't much to do but watch trashy TV while I was in the bed, so I spent some time doing just that. Dr. Hill came back and forth as she checked on the other patients and being bored to tears, I found myself eavesdropping where I could.

The man next to me had broken his foot after trying to change a hanging basket. The woman two beds down had accidentally put paint in her coffee instead of milk and had to have her stomach pumped. It was all morbidly fascinating, but the person that interested me the most was the short angry man in the bed opposite from me.

I glimpsed him briefly through the curtains as Dr. Hill went into talk with him and recognized him as the small angry man I had seen in the drugstore. My witchy intuition was buzzing for some reason, and I muttered a spell under my breath, one that would improve my hearing.

"Auditus."

Suddenly the sounds of the ward became brighter, louder, and clearer. In some ways it made it harder to hear because the background noise was so much louder, but I recalled that the spell worked on focus. I stared at the curtain ahead of me and sure enough the surrounding sound drowned out. The voice of Dr. Hill and the short patient became clearer.

"…but the fact of the matter is that we have to get it out Mr. Wood. Your feet are infected, and the medicine isn't working. You've already left this too long. What did you say happened again?"

"What?" Mr. Wood said in his gruff voice. "Oh, ah... I dropped a stained-glass fruit bowl in the kitchen. It was dark and I ended up having to walk through the broken glass barefoot. Look, I can get this out myself, just give me the good antibiotics."

"Antibiotics aren't going to do anything for you. We have to extract the glass, and you can't do it yourself, if this is about health insurance—"

"Don't have it, can't afford it, just give me the good painkillers and I'll be on my way!" he snapped.

"We have options to help with the costs," Dr. Hill said. "You're not listening to me. The hospital can pay for this, all you have to do is sign a few forms and—"

"And find myself in debt?! Ha! Not a chance!"

"I don't want to do this," she said. "But I have the capacity to do this with or without your permission. If we leave this much longer you will die, I—"

"Forget it!" he roared, loud enough that I would hear him without my spell. "I'm getting out of this scam hole, and don't you dare lay a finger on me!"

"Mr. Wood, I strongly advise you don't walk right now!"

"Don't tell me what to—argh!"

The small angry man suddenly came crashing through the curtain around his bed and slammed onto the floor. He rolled around on the floor in agony. He was wearing a gown, and his feet were wrapped in bloody bandages. Dr. Hill crouched to the floor to try and calm him, speaking into a phone as she did so.

"I need help on Ward 4. We have an unruly patient who needs an emergency procedure. He's not cooperating."

A team of orderlies and nurses came through the doors a moment later. They hoisted the roaring Mr. Wood onto a bed and wheeled him off the ward and out the doors, presumably somewhere to a place they could perform his operation in private.

Dr. Hill brushed a strand of sweaty hair from her face, brushed herself off and started for the door. I found myself calling after her.

"Doctor?" I said. She turned and looked at me.

"Is everything okay Miss Sponks?"

"I'm fine. I'm sorry, but I couldn't help overhearing, does that man have glass in his feet?"

She looked at me. "I'm not allowed to discuss such things with other patients, sorry."

"I understand, but well... I'm starting to piece something together. I need to make a quick call to the Sheriff to confirm something, and if my suspicions are correct, I will need you to make sure that man doesn't go anywhere after his operation."

She looked confused. "I'm afraid I don't follow. You think Mr. Wood's injuries are related to a crime?"

I nodded. "If my suspicions are correct then I think you might have a murderer on your hands."

The doctor suddenly paled. "Make that call, Miss Sponks. If you're correct, then I would like the police here straight away."

I grabbed my phone from off the bedside table and called Deacon, who answered almost immediately.

"Chelsea, is everything okay?"

"Everything's fine, but I need you to check something for me. It's about the Zaza case."

"I'm just at home looking over the notes right now," he said. "What do you need to know?"

"Jeez Deacon, burning the midnight oil much?"

"You called me to talk about the case!" he said, pointing out my hypocrisy.

"Fair enough, you have me there. Look, the Stark brothers said there was really only one clue at the scene, a broken window and blood on the floor."

"That's right," he said. "And?"

"I never saw the window in question, but in my ignorance, I assumed it was a plain glass window. It's not though, is it?"

"No. it's not. I went to the scene today after you left. It's a small stained glass window. Quite the piece really. You know that entire museum is a piece of art within itself—"

"Focus, Deacon. That's all I had to hear. There's a man here on my ward and get this—he has shards of stained glass in his feet. I bumped into him a couple of days ago at the drugstore, now he's gone for an emergency operation!"

"Hot diggety. All we have to do is match the glass in his feet to the window, and the blood at the crime scene to him! I'll send someone over straight away, so we have an officer stationed. Hey, this might even give me a reason to sleep in the chair next to your bed!"

"That's very sweet, but you don't have to do that, thank you. See you in the morning."

"See you in the morning, honey. Sleep well."

Like I had any chance of sleeping tonight!

When the morning rounds came about, I was dressed and ready to hop out of bed. Once I was discharged Deacon and I ran down the hall to a private room that had been set aside for the small angry man. The Stark brothers were both stationed outside, arguing back and forth with one another as we came around the corner.

"That's where you're dead wrong," Clark—or Mark, I still couldn't tell—said to his brother. "Aragorn was a master warrior. He could use a bow better than Legolas could use a sword."

"Get real!" the other twin replied. "Aragorn is a great swordsman, but he's useless with a bow and arrow. And look at Legolas, he's multi-faceted, the blade comes as easily to him as the bow and—"

"Keeping busy gentleman?" Deacon said as we reached the door. They were both so absorbed in their conversation they genuinely hadn't seen us approach. It was comforting to know that we had Pendle Island's finest guarding a murder suspect.

"Deacon!" they both said together and then, "Chelsea!"

"Has anyone been in or out of this door, Mark?" I asked.

"It's Clark actually, and no. The suspect in question is still sleeping from his op last night. It's all secure."

"As you were," Deacon said as he opened the door. I walked in and he followed me through. I was relieved to see that our suspect was still asleep in bed and hadn't in fact jumped out the window and done a runner. Mr. Wood began to stir as Deacon shut the door behind us.

"I said I didn't want breakfast or a wakeup call!" he barked. "I—oh," the small angry man suddenly opened his eyes wide upon seeing a policeman and myself in his room. "I know you," he said, scowling at me, and not making any effort to sit up at all. "You're the one from the paper. The detective."

"My fame knows no bounds," I said as I wandered into the room. "We ran into each other in the drugstore, do you remember? I thought you seemed a little jumpy when you saw me."

"I thought you'd followed me in there," he said.

"That explains why you were so twitchy. So, I take it you know why we're here?"

The small angry man let out a long and defeated sigh. "I didn't mean to kill him. I just wanted that statue. How was I supposed to know he'd be in there?"

"You don't have to tell us this," Deacon said. "You have the right to a lawyer."

"Pah, lawyers! Blood sucking vampires the lot of them! You think I'll be paying for a lawyer?! Why is everyone always trying to rip me off?!"

"You have a right to a public defender," Deacon said. "Should you be unable to afford your own legal representation."

"I might as well just tighten the noose around my own neck. They're all criminals."

"You literally murdered someone," I reminded him.

"It was an accident, get off your high horse! I broke in through the window and had the statue in my hands. That toff came through the door and scared the life out of me! I reacted on instinct!"

"You hit him with the statue," I said. "That was the murder weapon?"

"Sure was. Blooming heavy too. Didn't realize it would kill the poor bloke. Just wanted to knock him out."

"How on earth did you get glass in your feet?" Deacon said.

"What? Oh, well. I took my shoes off before I entered the museum grounds. Didn't want to leave distinctive tread patterns or anything like that. I've seen enough of those crime shows to know that some evidence is always left behind. I'm smart like that."

"Yes, it's clearly paying off big time," I said. "What did you do with the statue?"

"It's stashed at my house," he said with another sigh. "How long am I looking at here?"

Deacon and I looked at one another. "We're just investigating and charging you Mr. Wood, the court handles the verdict and sentencing."

He scowled. "It better not take too long, my tax dollars pay your salary!"

"Not for long," I muttered under my breath. I cleared my throat. "That solves Zaza's murder then, but what about Verity Newport. Why did you kill her?"

"Who?"

"Verity Newport," Deacon repeated. "Zaza's girlfriend. She turned up dead two days ago."

Mr. Wood just stared between us, looking utterly lost. "I have no idea what you're talking about."

"And me?" I said. "What did you stand to gain from killing me?"

"What are you talking about?!" he snapped, his confusion now giving way to his temper.

Deacon shifted. "The clocktower. You told Chelsea to meet you there and pushed her down the stairs. That's how she ended up in hospital."

"Excuse me officer, but are you as dumb as you look? I can't even walk since the beginning of this week! Why would I try and kill this idiot, or anyone else?! I already told you this business with the art guy was a mistake!"

"He has a point, Deacon," I said. "I saw him try and leave last night. He couldn't even walk out of here."

"Look," Mr. Wood said, "I know you both think I'm stupid, I can see it in your snobbish college eyes."

"I never went to college," Deacon said.

"Me neither."

"Just shut up!" Mr. Wood snapped. "Why on earth would I admit to one murder and not another? I have nothing to hide here, I know what I did was wrong, and I'm not going to waste your time. I killed the art guy, that was a mistake and boy, do I regret it. My dogs are killing me. But this girl, and this other one you're accusing me of killing? Not me. I swear my life on it."

Deacon looked at me. "Something tells me he's telling the truth."

"Me too," I said with a note of dissatisfaction. "Rats."

We had one murderer, but another was still out there.

This case was far from over.

13

"*W*here to, captain?!" Glenda hollered from the wheel, her tires screeching as her car screamed out of the hospital parking lot. I might have reached a momentary impasse with the Zaza case, but I still had plenty of other things to keep me busy, like saving my friend Adam from the literal jaws of death.

"Back to the shifter ranch. I have some unfinished business."

"Yee haw!" she hollered. "A hunting date with my big bad alpha. I think this guy is the one you know Chelsea," Glenda said, looking over at me while she ate strawberry laces right out of the packet. Her other hand was on the wheel, narrowly avoiding collision after collision as she wove in and out of lanes.

"Can you keep your eyes on the road?!" I said to her.

"A real driver uses *all* their senses when they're behind the wheel. Don't you worry about me. Glenda's been driving for fifteen years and she's never had a—" My aunt swung the car wildly to the left to avoid a station wagon coming our way. "Hey, bozo! I'm driving here!"

"You *were* in his lane," I said to her.

"Yeah maybe that one was my fault." Glenda tore another chuck off strawberry lace from the packet. "Want some?" she said, her mouth full and chewing.

"Let's just get to the ranch," I said. "I've already cheated death once this week. I don't need you to drive me right back to him."

Glenda somehow completed another car journey without wiping out half the town. She skidded onto the gravel path outside the ranch and I quickly exited the vehicle, cursing myself for getting in her car once again.

Note to self. Sort a car out by the end of next week.

We approached the gate to the ranch and Dean, the shifter that regularly guarded the entrance, appeared out of thin air.

"Stop right there," he said to the pair of us. "Where do you think you're going?"

"Into the ranch..." I said. I held up my hand to show him the ring, the one that granted me access at all times. "Harper gave me this. Remember?"

"He gave it to *you*," he said to me. "Last I checked you weren't allowed in," he said, looking at Glenda.

"What?!" Glenda said between mouthfuls of strawberry laces. "You little yellow belly pup! What's the matter, your 'alpha' afraid I'm going to school him on woodwork some more?!"

"I'm just following the rules," Dean said, looking back at me. "You're welcome to come in if you want. *She* will have to stay outside though."

"That's fine," I said. "Glenda, just wait in the car for twenty minutes or something. This is going to be a quick visit, I promise. I just need to talk to a few people."

"Fine," she said while rolling her eyes. "Maybe I can find a good tree and practice my axe throwing." Glenda scowled at Dean before walking back down the path.

Dean stepped aside and opened the gate. As I walked through the shifter ranch appeared before my eyes. This time I was immediately met with a welcoming party consisting of one man and three women. I was a little taken aback by the sudden attention and let out a nervous laugh.

"Um, hi!" I said. "Is the reception for me?"

"Greetings," a large man with sandy hair said as he extended his hand. He was another buff lumberjack type, an unassuming temple of strength lurking behind a quiet country boy exterior. "My name is Gerard, soon to be the new alpha here in Laika."

The three women alongside him introduce themselves in turn. "Rachel," said a short curvy woman with long dark curls.

"The detective! Ooh! I'm Sabine." Sabine was a tall willowy girl with silver hair.

"Goldie," said the final girl. She perhaps was the most imposing of them all, with a striking flawlessness that was almost irritating. With long red curls and her bright yellow shifter eyes she looked like a siren. "It's good to meet you. We heard you had been poking around."

"Poking around," I said. "Why do people always use that word to describe me? Like I'm some sort of rat lurking in the undergrowth."

They all laughed. "I would hope as shifters we could sniff out any rats," Gerard said, "but alas, it seems we have some trouble in our small town. I heard that Harper has employed you to help figure out the trouble with our chalice. Any luck?"

"I've made some progress, but no sign of the chalice yet. As it stands, I was actually looking to talk with each one of you, perhaps gain some insight as to what is going on around here."

"That is why we are here," Gerard said. "We are keen to get to the bottom of this quickly. No offense, but it causes great unrest to have people in this ranch that aren't wolfkin. We like to stay amongst our own."

"Well, let me ask you all some quick questions then. Who wants Melody out of the picture?"

"I beg your pardon?" Gerard said with a note of confusion.

"Adam and Melody are not acting like themselves, which is in part because they are drugged. Nadine, Melody's sister found the remains of a magical orb, one designed to make its target act… loopy."

Gerard laughed. "Miss Sponks I can assure you that no one here knows anything about magic. Wolfkin do not align themselves with such methods."

"Maybe it was you?" I said to Gerard. "Remove Melody from the picture so she's not voted in as your mate. According to Nadine she was a shoe in for the pack vote. But what if you're actually in love with one of the other three nominees? Rachel, Sabine, or Goldie?" The four looked among themselves and all burst into laughter. "Did I... say something funny?"

"Maybe you don't understand the ways of our kind, Miss Sponks," Sabine said. "But Gerard would quite happily take Melody as his queen bride over us."

"Someone will have to clear this up for me."

Gerard himself took the honor. "Sabine and I have already had a relationship. She is my ex. The same goes for Rachel."

"Okay..."

"Don't get us wrong," Rachel said. "We love Gerard, but I do *not* want to be his mate forever. I'm sure Sabine and Goldie would agree."

"Amen to that!" said Gerard.

"And you?" I said to Goldie.

"Gerard is a competent leader, but we will not make good mates. We find each other very irritating. He is... how do you say, arrogant."

"And you're in love with yourself," Gerard scowled.

"So, you really do want Melody as your mate," I said to Gerard.

"That is the most preferable outcome for the whole pack."

"And none of you want to be the pack queen."

"No, not really. This is just ceremony," Rachel said. "Gerard has already been chosen, and Melody is the best fit for him. Maybe one day I will be a queen with an alpha that isn't so messy."

The four of them laughed.

"I hope this conversation has been helpful?" Gerard said.

"Well I've gone to suspecting it was one of you, to having no idea, so no, not really. But I guess in a way, yes. Thank you. Now if you don't mind me, I have to go and speak with my friend."

I said goodbye to Gerard and the girls and made my way through Laika to the townhall at the back. I decided to stop in at the workshop first and see Harper, but when I got there he wasn't around.

Something on his workbench did catch my eye though, and I wondered over to see a sculpted wooden heart on the table, with the initials 'GS' carved into the surface in billowy letters.

"GS?" I whispered to myself. *Glenda Sponks!* "Oh mercy, Glenda. How do you do it?"

"Can I help you?" Harper said. I jumped at his voice and turned around to see him standing in the doorway.

"Sorry," I said. "I just swung by to say hello."

Harper hurried over and took the heart from off the table, putting it into a cabinet on the wall behind him. For the brief second the cabinet was open I saw a flash of something red inside. "I can see that," he said. "Have you made any progress?"

"I think I have. I know why Adam and Melody are acting so strange."

"Oh?" he said, his brow furrowing interest. "Why's that?"

"Magical interference. But I have an antidote, so we can set them straight right away."

"Magic? I think you have the wrong end of the stick. No one around here uses magic."

"Well someone did. A small thing called an orb of inhibition. It's like a small smoke bomb, and it leaves the victims to act like they're drunk for almost a week."

"I see," Harper said, his jaw tensing in thought. "And how did you come to this conclusion?"

"Nadine brought me one. She found it on the floor in the cells."

"The culprit must have dropped it," Harper said.

"Exactly."

"And after this antidote, will they be able to tell us who drugged them in the first place?"

"No, but I'll have my friend back, and you'll have your sister. With a clear mind Adam might even tell us where the chalice is."

Harper grinned. "Well that's brilliant. But what about the culprit? How do we find out who spiked them in the first place?"

"According to my familiar they would need—" I stopped myself suddenly, my witchy intuition itching at the back of my neck. Artemis said the little magical orbs were easy to make. Just some poppies and a little spite magic. An idea came to me though.

"They would need pine needles to make the magical item, and

probably a gas mask to prevent them from spiking themselves." A stern expression suddenly turned on Harper's face. "What is it?" I asked.

"Pine needles? Are you sure?"

"That's right. Anyway. I'll go administer the antidote. We're one step closer to your pack moving on with the ceremony."

"Perfect. You treat the drunken lovers. I would like to check on something quickly and then I will report back here. I think I might know who our culprit is."

"You want me to come with you?" I asked.

"No, make sure Adam and Melody are okay first. I just want to check something. We will uncover the culprit together when my sister is healed."

Harper waited for me to move first and followed me out of the workshop. He closed the door behind me and locked it. "I'll be right back. I'll meet you down in the cells."

I watched the large man quickly hurry down the hall and out of sight. As soon as he was gone, I turned on my heels, pulled my wand from my pocket and poked the tip into the keyhole. I didn't actually know any spells for opening locks off the top of my head, but I tried something anyway.

"Hey," I said, looking down at my wand. "Can you open this door?"

My wand was a pretty little thing, carved entirely from wood, with three distinct strands woven around so that it looked like three twigs braided together. I don't know what possessed me to try talking to it, but to my surprise I saw a miniature face appear in the grain, two eyes and a mouth that moved as it talked back.

"Oh... I suppose so," it said in a voice that was deep and sleepy.

All of a sudden the wand fizzed and a jolt of light came out the tip and into the door. The lock clicked and the door swung open. I glanced nervously over my shoulder before rushing inside the workshop.

"All right Chelsea, time to poke around like the rat you are," I muttered to myself. I know what I wanted to look for first. My feet took me straight to the cabinet where Harper had stashed his wooden heart. I opened it and saw the sculpture, along with a pile of dried poppies.

Harper!

On the shelf underneath that was the hold all bag I saw Rudy bring to the ranch the first night I came here. I looked inside and saw a little mountain of the glittering red orbs of inhibition, along with a gas mask. There was a note folded inside.

Harper,

Here's the stuff you wanted. Be careful with these little guys, they last a while! I also made you some orbs of clarity to remove the effects of the spell once your ceremony is over. Hope you guys have fun getting messed up on these things, just party safe!

Rudy.

"So, Rudy was the supplier," I muttered to myself. From the looks of things Rudy didn't know that Harper was using the magical items with ill intent.

There was more. On the inside door of the cabinet there was a picture of Goldie, the shifter woman I had met outside, held in place with a pin. Behind the photo there was another note.

Harper,

I don't care if you're the big bad alpha. I already told you I'm not interested. Nothing is going to happen between us, so please stop with the advances. I give you this photo in hopes that you will leave me alone. Jerk.

Goldie.

"Huh," I said to myself as I put the note back. The pieces were starting to fall into place. I quickly closed the cabinet door and rushed out of the workshop, closing the door behind myself as I left. "Time to free Adam."

As I walked to the stairs leading to the cells, I crossed paths with Nadine. "Oh! I was looking for you Chelsea!" she said. "Gerard said he and the girls just met you."

"Yes, I believe we might have a solution to this riddle after all."

"You do? That's brilliant! Harper just rushed past me. He said he had something important to do."

Covering his tracks perhaps?

"I bet he does," I said. "Anyway, I'm going to give Adam and Melody the antidote. Do you want to come?"

"Sure!"

Nadine and I both went down into the cells. I wasn't surprised to see Melody there once again, talking to Adam through the bars. The pair of them looked like a couple of lovesick teenagers. It was cute in a yucky kind of way.

"Hey lovebirds," I said. They both looked my way.

"Oh Chelsea!" Melody sang. "You're back! Help us settle a debate. Hawaii or Scotland for our honeymoon?!"

"Hawaii, obviously," I said, fishing Artemis' antidote out of my pocket. I was about to hurl the little orb at the ground when I stopped myself, remembering how he had turned himself supersized off the back of an invisibility potion.

"What's the matter?" Nadine asked.

"I'm just wondering if I can trust my familiar to come through for me. I have little other option I guess." I looked at Melody and Adam. "Sorry to break up the party guys."

With that I hurled the little orb and it burst on the floor, filling the room and corridors with glittering green smoke. It smelled like mint and linen. When the smoke cleared, I was relieved to see that everything looked normal, which meant there were no immediate unexpected side effects.

Melody and Adam were both blinking, their faces a picture of confusion and gratitude.

"Oh, finally!" Adam said, standing up from his stool to take a deep breath. "I am me again!"

Melody was clutching her head in her hands, looking equally as relieved as Adam. "Chelsea, I cannot thank you enough!"

The white-haired sister rushed towards me and smothered me in a hug.

"Not a big hugger," I wheezed through her death grip, "but thanks. You're both feeling better then?"

"Oh man, you have no idea what it's been like!" Adam said. "I was aware of myself the whole time, but I couldn't stop myself from acting stupid!"

"Yes," Melody said. "Exactly like that. I couldn't stop myself, but—" She paused and looked at Adam. "Adam… everything I said about you is true. I really do feel that way."

"Me too," he said, a warm smile filling his face. He looked at me and his expression straightened. "The creaky bed in your basement."

"…What about it?"

"I stuffed the chalice under the mattress. It's hidden there."

"That explains the bumpy mattress then. Artemis said you wouldn't remember who threw the orb in the first place. Any chance he was wrong?"

They both shook their heads. "No, I don't remember." Melody said.

"Me neither," Adam added.

"It doesn't matter. Harper is about to burst in here and tell us he's figured everything out. I think we'll need some sort of village meeting too."

"What, really?" Nadine asked.

"I'm… fifty percent sure."

Sure enough Harper ran down the stairs to the cells only a moment later. "Chelsea, you won't believe this, I've got our culprit. I've summoned everyone to the village square."

"Brilliant, you saved me a job. Let's go up at once. Everyone now. Hurry up. I still have business to attend to back in my normal life."

Nadine opened Adam's cell and we all followed Harper upstairs and outside into the square. There a hundred men and women were all congregated in a wide circle. Most of them I didn't know, but I recognized Dean, Gerard, and the three prospective brides.

"Let's cut to the chase," Harper announced loudly, his voice booming through the forest. "Someone has been trying to tear apart our community, and with the help of Chelsea here I've managed to get to the bottom of it. Recently Adam took the chalice from us—" Harper paused as the crowd broke into disapproving boos. "But it came to our attention he was not at fault. He and my sister Melody were both drugged with magic, made to act in ways that they normally wouldn't. Chelsea here figured that out, and she has also cured them both."

"So, who was it, Harper?" I asked. "You found the suspected pine needles and gas mask?"

"That I did," he announced gravely. "In the cabin of none other than our successive Alpha, Gerard." Harper turned and faced the upcoming leader. "Guards, seize him."

A number of shifter men moved forward from the crowd and seized Gerard, who didn't put up much of a fight. He didn't even look mad, just confused.

"Harper?" He laughed. "What are you talking about? Why would I do this?"

"To delay the ceremony," Harper said. "To delay the unification with Melody."

"And why would I want to do a thing like that?"

"Because you're in love with Goldie," I said to Gerard. "Oops, wait." I turned and faced Harper. "I meant to say that to you. You're the one in love with her after all."

"I—what?" the alpha said, his jaw clenching tight as I interrupted him.

"The spell isn't crafted with pine needles," I said. "It's crafted with poppies, just like the ones I saw in that cabinet back in your workshop. You already knew that of course, I just needed to get you out of that workshop for five minutes so I could find the real evidence, which is hidden in your locker. I knew you were desperate enough to pin this on someone else, and I was right."

"I—This is slander!" Harper growled through his teeth. "Guards! Seize her too! The witch must be working with the betrayer!"

"Just hang on a sec puppers," I said, holding my wand out in the direction of the advancing guards. "I'll have you know I'm a very advanced witch, a level nine spellcaster. Take another step and I'll turn this entire town into a bowl of giant raspberry custard."

The guards froze, seemingly terrified by my bluff.

"I'll admit it took me too long to piece it together Harper, but perhaps I should have looked a little closer at you. You spiked Adam because you needed someone outside of your pack to take the chalice. He'd been hanging around trying to sweet talk Melody, so he was the perfect candidate. But why drug your own sister? Well, the answer is obvious too. She was pretty much already established as Gerard's mate, but you didn't like that idea, did you?"

Harper just stared at me, hate blazing in those bright shifter eyes. "Stop spinning your lies, witch. Guards, seize her!"

The guards didn't. I was glad to see that my threat of custard oblivion had them scared out of their wits. I couldn't take on an entire pack of shifter guards on my own.

"After talking with Gerard and the girls I realized that none of them had anything to gain from interfering with the ceremony. In fact, the only person that did was… you. With Melody acting weird and no chalice, the ceremony would have to be delayed. And by making Gerard look guilty you could rule him out of the running too. I'm guessing with him out of the picture you could put yourself forward as leader again and get yourself a new mate in the process. I'm guessing your heart was already set on someone, someone like Goldie. Maybe you thought she would see you in a different light once you managed to extend your leadership?"

Goldie stepped forward from the crowd. "Harper, is this true? You did all this just to try and win me over? I already told you I am not into you. You are like… ten years too old for me. It's not going to happen. Ever."

"What's your last name?" I asked. "Something beginning with S?"

"Shepard," she said.

"GS." Goldie Shepard. Not Glenda Sponks. "That heart in your workshop is for Goldie. There's a bag in your locker stuffed full of the suspect magical orbs. You asked Rudy Malkin for his assistance, you told him it was entirely recreational, something to do with your ceremony. Little did he know your intentions were more insidious."

"I think I've heard enough of these lies, witch!"

With that Harper launched forward through the air, taking on the form of a humongous snarling wolf as he jumped right at me. I had no time to react at all and was almost certainly dead, but a blur flew from the right and knocked Harper to the side. All at once shifter men and women took on the form of giant wolves, quickly surrounding Harper in a circle and protecting me from him.

"Well, there you have it!" I said, my voice a little shaken from adrenaline. "Mystery solved!"

"Guards!" Gerard shouted. "Unhand me and seize him," They did as he said and apprehended Harper. "Everyone, back to your business!"

The wolf that knocked Harper out of the air shifted back into his human form. It was Dean, the annoying guard that watched over the entrance to Laika. "Witch, are you okay?" he said.

"Thanks to you, yes," I said. "I owe you one, Dean."

"Please, do not commit yourself to the idea of any sort of debt, witch," he frowned. "I do not want such a close association with a human."

"You came so close to not acting like a jerk," I said.

He smiled. "Forgive me, it's hard sometimes to trust people outside of my own kind. "Thank you for saving our pack. The gratitude is all mine." Dean turned and walked away. I couldn't be sure, but I felt like we'd almost ended on being friends.

"Chelsea! That was amazing!" Melody said as she ran over to me. She lowered her voice to a whisper. "Are you really a level nine witch?"

"I don't even know if there are levels Melody, I just made that up. I thought it sounded menacing."

"It definitely did," Adam said. "Those guards were terrified of you!"

"I guess I should extend my thanks," Gerard said as he came across to us. "Without your help Harper would still be the leader of this pack, and quite a few innocent people would be behind bars. I will have to ask for the ring back, and the chalice of course, but I formally extend a token of gratitude from the town of Laika to you. Should you ever need our assistance with something… don't hesitate to ask."

"Maybe I'll cash that in one straight away," I said to Gerard. "I might need help consoling my dear Aunt Glenda. She was convinced Harper was the one. This is the second time this month a betrothed of hers has been taken away in handcuffs."

Gerard swallowed at something in his throat. "Perhaps I shall add a caveat to that token of gratitude. We will help you with anything… as long as it doesn't concern your family."

"I think with sensible leadership like that this pack is in safe hands, Gerard." I said as I gave the ring back to him.

1 4

After giving back the ring I exited shifter ranch for the last time and found Glenda on the other side of the fence, waiting in her car. As I climbed into the car, I saw her swiping through profiles on a dating app.

"Too handsome. Too ugly. Too poor. Too rich!" She sighed and shoved her phone into her pocket. "Oh Chelsea, am I ever going to find *the one*?!"

"You're over Harper then? That's good because he was the one behind everything."

"Yeah I figured as much," she said as she started up the car and reversed back onto the main road. She put her foot down and we took off with a jolt. "He seemed too perfect, which should have raised my suspicions from the beginning. Your friend Adam is off the hook then?"

"He is. He's staying behind for a bit and talking with the new alpha Gerard. Adam is going to come over to the house later and give them back the chalice. He's hidden it there."

"Where do you want to go now then? Want to come watch Die Hard at the wool shop?"

"I think I'd like to just go home," I said. "It's been another crazy couple of days. I'm starting to think I'm never going to get any peace."

"Aw, shucks. Don't worry darling," Glenda said as she threw her car around another perilous corner. "I'll make sure you get home okay so you can relax."

"Thanks," I said, hissing through my teeth as I gripped the dashboard.

Witchy gods help me!

When we finally got home, Glenda said a brief goodbye before spinning off my driveway, her tires kicking up gravel as she sped away. I rolled my eyes and headed inside. The ever-ready pirate ghost of Old Mad John was nowhere to be seen as I made my way through the front door.

"Odd," I said. It wasn't often that he missed a chance to try and scare someone.

I hung up my jacket and bag in the hallway and went into the kitchen to see the old pirate ghost sat at the table with none other than Rudy Malkin, Selena, and the hamster-sized version of my familiar Artemis.

"Chelsea!" Selena said joyfully, jumping out of her chair to greet me. "You're home! Would you like some dinner? I made a meal from scratch!"

"I'm good thanks Selena," I said. "I'm not really in the mood for boot lasagna."

"Actually, I think I *am* on the mend. I made tacos, and Rudy here tells me that it's almost entirely normal!"

"Chelsea, you have to help!" Artemis said in his pixie-pitch voice. "Being small is terrible! The mice in the house have been torturing me nonstop!"

"Karma's a beach, eh, Artemis?" I looked at the dish of tacos on the kitchen side. "They do actually look quite good."

"I've never had tacos with sprinkles in them," Rudy said, sat half-turned with one arm on the back of his chair. "But I have to admit it. They work."

"And why are you in my house?" I said to him.

Rudy looked offended. "What? A friend can't come and say thanks to Pendle Island's most esteemed amateur investigator? If it wasn't for you those police would probably have locked me up already. You got me off the hook. And for that I say thanks."

"Don't take this the wrong way Rudy, but I still don't know if I can trust you or not. I just finished solving a bunch of trouble at shifter ranch, for which you were partly responsible."

"I am?" he said. "What did I do now?"

"Supplying magical items to Harper? Those orbs of inhibition you gave him, he was using them to control his sister and my friend."

Rudy stood up suddenly. "What? I told that idiot to be careful with them! He said they were for a ceremony!"

"Relax, it's sorted now. You really had no idea?"

"No, I wouldn't have given them to him otherwise. Honestly, I feel a bit stupid for trusting him in the first place. I figured as a leader he might be trustworthy."

"It took me some time to figure it out too. I'll admit, he played me well. So, what are you doing here?"

"I want to help," he said.

"With the case? Verity's murder is still under question."

"For which I have an alibi."

"True, I just don't understand it. She only contacted me to provide an alibi for you. But she was lying, wasn't she? You weren't with her that night."

He shook his head. "No, I wasn't. I went home after the museum like I said, and then I went to the shifter ranch. I don't know why Verity felt the need to lie for me, but I jumped on the opportunity as it got the police off my back."

"So why would she lie for you? Why go the length of making up an alibi for you?"

Rudy scratched his head. "I don't want to sound like I'm being big-headed here, but Verity always had a bit of a thing for me. I don't know if you've noticed, but the girls tend to throw themselves at me. Isn't that right, Selena?"

Selena made a face, looking like she'd smelled something bad.

"Ooh, yeah. Don't take this the wrong way, but you're not really my type."

Rudy laughed. "Ah, you like me, you just don't realize it yet." Rudy's phone started ringing, he pulled it out of his pocket and answered it. "Poppy? Hey. What's up? You'll have to speak up, your phone is doing that weird clicking thing again. Look, no. I don't need any more money. You shouldn't have paid me in the first place, Poppy, I, Poppy? You're breaking up again. I'll text you."

He ended the call and started typing out a text. For some reason I found the gears in my head turning over.

"Bad reception?" I asked him.

"Huh? Oh, yeah. Her phone is always like that. She got paint or something in it a few months back and it's been acting up ever since. It's really annoying, like this—"

"High-pitched clicking sound that echoes over the call."

"Yeah! How did you know? Have you talked with Poppy on the phone?"

"I didn't realize it until now, but yes, I guess I must have. That was the exact type of interference on the anonymous call that brought me to the old clock tower. Meaning—"

"That Poppy was the one that tried to kill you!" Rudy said.

"And if my money is in the right place, she's the one that killed Verity too. She must have caught wind of Verity's made up alibi and took it as the truth. Rage can make people act in strange ways."

"But why would Poppy get mad about me being with Verity?"

Everyone else at the table looked at each other. "Really? Numb nuts?" Artemis said.

"What?" Rudy asked.

"She has a thing for you, Rudy," I said. "That's why she paid you out of her own pocket. That's why she paid your bail. That's why she killed Verity when she caught wind that you were having a relationship together." I pulled my phone out and called Deacon.

"Yes, my darling?" he said down the line.

"Get the station together, Deacon. Poppy Chen is our missing puzzle piece. She killed Verity, and she tried to kill me too. I'm certain."

Deacon sighed down the phone. "I was just about to make nachos, but I guess they can wait."

"Make them for the road. We can eat them together in the car."

"Now that sounds like a plan!"

———

Poppy Chen confessed to everything when we confronted her at the hotel. The small Asian woman didn't even shed a tear as Mark and Clark led her into the back of the police car. My suspicions were entirely correct, and she'd killed Verity in a spat of blind rage. Poppy had overheard Verity make the call to me and followed her to the old warehouse the night Verity and I were meant to meet. Her emotions got the better of her and she snapped.

"Tell Rudy I love him!" Poppy said as Mark and Clark moved her into the car.

"Why don't you write him from prison?" I said.

Deacon laughed and shook his head. We both watched as the car pulled away from the hotel. Deacon yawned and I rested my head against his shoulder. It was late and we were the only ones left outside the front of the hotel.

"Well, you did it, Chelsea," he said. "Another case solved. Say, is it your magic that helps you figure all this out?"

"You know it might help a little, but most of the time it's just me being me. Why?"

"I know I've said it a few times, but I think you really could make a go of being a private investigator. You've clearly got a knack for this sort of thing. The department hasn't issued a license for a few years now, but we have the budget for it. Normally we train police, but there's nothing to stop us from taking a citizen on. It might be a bit more work for you, but I'm sure you can do it. Once you're officially trained it's a good source of income too, unless you have some sort of witchy job that I don't know about."

"Witchy job?" I asked. "Like what?!"

"I don't know, broom cleaner? Frog catcher? Potion maker? Are any of these things real?"

I laughed. "I'm not sure. But I wouldn't be surprised. Let me think about the investigator thing. I guess it makes sense. I'm not good at many things, but if I can make this skill of mine a little more profitable, I wouldn't have to worry about money so much." A big yawn escaped me. "Want to stay at my place tonight?"

"Is there any witchy stuff I should know about?"

"A miniature talking cat, I have a witch staying with me and she's a bit loopy, also my house is possessed by the ghost of an old mad pirate named Old Mad John. You've never been able to see him before, but now you know about magic that might be different."

"We could always stay at mine," he suggested.

"That might be best."

Suddenly the air filled with pink and green smoke. Deacon automatically went into protective boyfriend mode and jumped in front of me, his gun held up in the air to tackle the mysterious threat.

"Relax Deacon," I coughed over the smoke. "It's fine! It's just the Magic Police!"

We both coughed and swathed away the smoke to see Chad Chaplin stood on top of Deacon's car. He immediately blushed and jumped onto the sidewalk.

"Oops!" he said. "Sorry! Must have got my coordinates slightly wrong. Chelsea! And look, the human boyfriend!"

"What's going on here?" Deacon asked, slowly holstering his gun.

"Chad Chaplin, Junior Detective for the Magical Crimes Investigation. I was assigned to monitor the pair of you after you accidentally learned about Chelsea's magic."

"Junior Detective?" I asked. "I thought you were a Principle Warlock now or something."

"Warlock in Principis," he corrected. "And well... there might have been a slight mishap, which might have led to a minor *temporary* demotion."

"What did you do?" I asked.

"I might have accidentally turned an Archwizard into a toad. Permanently. It's a bit messy. He's not best pleased."

"You came here to tell us that?" I asked.

"What? No! I wanted to let you know that the case against you has been closed. You're both clear of any further surveillance. We've deemed that you are not a threat Mr. Long."

"Uh…thanks?" Deacon said uncertainly.

"We'd established that two days ago Chad," I said to the boy-faced detective, "but thanks for coming to tell us. Is there anything I can do to help with your toad problem?"

"Not really," he said. "They're quite impressed in a way. No one has ever seen anything like this before. They can't figure out what I've done. Anyway. I'll be off. I have a lot of paperwork to catch up on. I'm considering a career change. I always fancied myself as a dragon wrangler."

"Maybe stick to small time stuff for now, eh Chad? See you later."

"Bye!"

Chad disappeared in another obnoxious puff of smoke, leaving me and a confused Deacon on the sidewalk outside the hotel.

"There's still time for you to back out, you know," I said to Deacon. "I can appreciate this is all a bit much to take in."

"Why would I back out now?" he asked. "Things are just getting interesting."

"I guess I have a lot more baggage than a normal girl."

"Good thing you're cute then," he said as he leaned into kiss me. "Shall we go home?"

"That sounds like a good idea." I said and followed him over to the car. Maybe it was my imagination, but I thought it felt like things were finally going back to being peaceful.

How naïve I was.

*W*hen Deacon dropped me off at my house the next morning, we kissed goodbye and made plans to meet up again later that day. Old Mad John was missing once again as I opened the front door and when I walked into the kitchen to feed Artemis I realized why. The old pirate ghost was sat at the kitchen table with my mother. A mountain of candy pink suitcases were around the table and my mother was in a chair next to the pirate ghost, flirting unashamedly.

"Oh, you're such a tease!" she laughed, placing a hand on Old Mad John's ghostly leg.

"Get out!" he chuckled under his breath. Sounding both abashed and proud. I cleared my throat to make myself known.

"Ahem."

"Oh, Chelsea darling!" my mother said as she jumped out of her chair. "Come and give your old mother a kiss!" Mom skipped across the kitchen like a dressage horse and kissed the air on both sides of my face. "Oh, look at you, a homeowner! I'm so proud!"

"What happened to the call?" I said.

"I wanted to surprise you! And look how surprised you are! John has just been telling me all about you and your exploits, it sounds like you've been rather busy since you got back on the island!"

"It's *Old Mad John*, mom, and yeah, things have been a bit hectic. He's a ghost by the way, you can't start a relationship with him."

"Not again, anyway!" she cackled.

I looked at the pirate ghost and narrowed my eyes in confusion. "Wait, you guys—"

"No need to drag up the past darling!" Mom laughed, stepping in front of my eyeline to make sure the attention stayed on her. "Actually, I did come back to the island for a reason. Now you know about your witchy upbringing I figured it was only fair to clue you in on a few more secrets about your past. Also, we never spend time together anymore! It might be good to settle down for a month and just really get to know one another again!"

"A month?" I croaked.

"Of course, we have a lot of work to get done here," she said. "This house could use a fresh lick of paint. You know real estate is a valuable investment, Chelsea, and you have to stay on top of it."

"I've had some issues with a tumultuous houseguest," I said. "I have been—"

"But we'll get to all that in time. We've already got quite a bit to do this morning. Our guest should be here any minute, and we have so much catching up to do!"

"Guest?" I said. "You've only just got here and you're inviting people around!"

"Relax darling. It's just family, and it's part of the reason I wanted to come back here. I never gave you a chance to discover your roots. Family is the most important thing in the world after all!"

Just then a knock came at the front door. I had no idea what my mom was talking about, but I twirled out of her embrace and went into the hall to get the door. I opened the door to find Rudy Malkin.

"What on earth are you doing here?" I asked.

A puzzled Rudy looked back at his bike. "Sorry. I must have put the wrong address into my GPS. I'm meant to be meeting someone."

He rubbed his eyes and yawned. "Bit of a long night. I was up party-ing. I just got a text from someone interested in discussing my artwork."

"That's great. If you don't mind, I'm in the middle of something here. Trust me, you don't want to get caught up in this. Just get out while you—"

"Rudolph!" My mother sang, skipping out onto the porch to throw her arms around Rudy Malkin. "How are you darling?!"

Rudy sobered up immediately, catching my mother in a hug that he quickly pushed himself out of. He took a step back on the porch, staring at my mother as if he'd just seen a ghost.

"What are you doing back here?" he scowled at her.

"Darling I've come back to the island!" she said. "I'm living my best life. Sorry about the little bit of dishonesty. I am dying to see your artwork, but I'm probably not buying today! I couldn't think of another way to get you to meet with me." She laughed.

"I'm sorry," I said. "What in the ever-loving turkey is going on here?"

"Well I thought it was about time you both met!" Mom said. "I've been wanting to introduce you both for years!"

"We already know each other," I said. "Mom, what is going on?"

Rudy turned and looked at me. "Wait, what did you just say? This woman is your mother?"

"Of course I am, Rudolph. Not all children emancipate themselves the second they get a chance!"

"Like you gave me any other choice," Rudy hissed.

"Wait," I said, the cogs rapidly turning in my head. I looked at Rudy and froze. "You—"

"Let me clear the air!" Mom sang. "Chelsea, Rudy here is your brother. And you're his sister!"

"Wait, what?!" Rudy said.

"Wait, what?!" I repeated.

. . .

Witchy gods save me!

Click here to get book 5 'Old Witch New Tricks' available now.

THANKS FOR READING

Thanks for reading, I hope you enjoyed the book.

It would really help me out if you could leave an honest review with your thoughts and rating on Amazon. Every bit of feedback helps!